THE MOST BORING CHRISTMAS SPECIAL EVER WRITTEN

An adventure-less and almost choice-less pick-your-path novella

Rudolf Kerkhoven

THANK YOU, ERIN. I KNOW IT WAS BORING.

This is somewhat of a **sequel** to a novella called
*The Most **Boring** Book Ever Written.*
No person can be blamed
for having **never read it**.
It has a lot of **one-star** reviews.

All one needs to know is that
You used to be in the Air Force,
but are now a commercial airline **pilot**.

Also,

Ann is your wife
Emma is your daughter
Liam is your son
That is **it**.

■ ■ ■

Now this is something to be excited about: just in time for the holidays, limited edition cans of Cranberry 7-Up! The design of the packaging is simple but unquestionably effective. A single, perky cranberry has replaced the distinctive and gleaming red circle in the middle of the iconic 7-Up logo. Well done, graphic designers (although, to be honest, you initially thought that these were 12-packs of Cherry 7-Up, a fantastic product that seems to have been discontinued in your jurisdiction, presumably because of lackluster sales; are the people of this city so boring that they can't accept a little variety in their lives?). You appreciate the tart bite of a cranberry and look forward to how it will inevitably complement the sweet, citrus notes of traditional 7-Up. And, if you're not mistaken, cranberries are a super-food, rich with antioxidants. Much like the ever-versatile parsnip, this product might very well be both delicious *and* healthful. You pick up the lengthy box, conveniently shaped to take advantage of a refrigerator's depth. While you feel that there are many things about modern life that have failed to offer substantial improvements over the living conditions of your younger years, the "refrigerator pack" is definitely a worthwhile invention.

You then sigh, pondering this last thought. Holding up the package with just two fingers snug within the perforated opening, you wonder if it is really fair to call this an *invention?* Is it not just a rectangular prism made of flimsy cardboard? And yet, this still feels like a more substantial offering to civilization than so many modern innovations. Like bike-lanes on busy roads. Or Snapchat. Not that you really know what Snapchat is. But Emma keeps referencing it— or to be honest, you hear Emma referencing it when she is amongst

3

her friends. A colleague recently informed you that although Snapchat began as a way for adolescent boys to transmit self-destructing images of their penises, it is now much more innocuous. People can send photographs of their faces with superimposed dog ears or rainbow vomit. You shake your head and turn the 12-pack around in one hand. Yes, compared to Snapchat (or those darn bike-lanes), a square-based rectangular prism made of cardboard is a superior innovation. Sorry, Wright Brothers, but this is the world we now live in. And what if Emma is getting inundated with shots of pre-adolescent genitals? Would she inform you of this? Would you want to know? Do nine-year-old boys take pleasure in such things?

Anyhow, there is no more time for trivial thoughts. Your annual Christmas Eve appie party awaits. If you dawdle at this grocery store any longer, Ann will soon accuse you of deliberately wasting time. She is always criticizing you of this, which you find annoying for several reasons—most important of which being that it is entirely true, hence rendering your attempts at refuting such accusations as weak and uninspired. The edge of the cardboard handle is digging into the crooks of your fingers and you try putting the box of Cranberry 7-Up into your grocery basket, but there is no way you can fit it without crushing the bread. This really shouldn't be a problem; back in the military, you would be forced to carry fifty-pound backpacks on arduous and trying hikes along rain soaked trails. You used to be in amazing shape, always eager to take off your shirt when playing beach volleyball with the boys on a hot summer day. Now, you try to stay clothed at all times, ashamed of what has happened to your once-toned torso. Now, it is the mass of a 12-pack of soda that you find arduous and trying.

So, with the black plastic basket in one hand and the festive-themed box of soda in the other, you walk towards the checkouts while surveying the products you've acquired: a loaf of bread (loaded with flax seeds, of course), a 12-ounce plastic tub of cream cheese

(Philadelphia brand, of course), a jar of chili pepper jelly (for the hors d'oeuvres, of course), a box of Triscuits (family-sized, of course), a bag of rolled oats (Quaker brand, of course), what you estimate to be a couple pounds of potatoes (for baked potato skins, of course), a pack of Trojan condoms, (Magnum, of course).

Wait! A pack of condoms? What is that doing in there? You didn't get these. You then remember a group of adolescent males walking down the aisles mere minutes earlier. They were snickering while passing by and you assumed this to be a symptom of whatever intoxicant teenagers abide in these days. Now you realize that those boys must have placed this box of condoms into your basket. And worst of all, you don't have a free hand to remove the offending package. After looking around to see if these hooligans were still in sight, you put down the pack of Cranberry 7-Up and withdraw the glossy box. But where to put such a thing? You are standing by an assortment of dried fruit and this does not seem to be an appropriate place to cast aside contraceptives. With a disgruntled sigh, you leave the condoms beside a pack of Sun-Maid Raisins and prepare to walk away while no one is watching.

But first you add a bag of Sun-Maid Raisins to your basket. Everyone loves a few raisins, you think to yourself. And combined with the rolled oats that you have already acquired, this would ensure that Ann makes even more of your favorite oatmeal-raisin cookies. So, yes, definitely less than the nine-item maximum required to utilize the express checkout. You turn the corner, ready to select the optimal line.

Crap.

There are only three tills open, none of which being an express-lane, and all of which extend several customers deep. You let out a long, deflating groan. "What a disaster," you say with a throaty sigh.

"What?" a man asks as he emerges from the corner, pushing a cart with nothing but a pair of frozen turkeys. Fool, you think.

There is no way that those turkeys are going to defrost in time for tomorrow.

Unless he's Jewish. Then the fact that it is Christmas Day tomorrow would not matter. He could roast his turkey(s) on the 26th.

"Sorry?" You say, unsure what the man was asking you about.

"I didn't mean to eavesdrop, but you said something about a disaster. Did something happen?"

"Oh, no. Just that." You point towards the lines of people slumped over their carts, burdensome baskets nudged forward on the floor with prodding feet, impatient children spinning around weary parents. "I was hoping to get out of here quickly. But it looks like all the lines are slow. This is going to take a while."

"Oh," the man is noticeably relieved. "I thought you meant, like, an actual disaster."

You nod, knowing exactly what the man is talking about. "Like credit and debit not being accepted?"

The man's thick, black eyebrows furrow. You start to wonder if he's not Jewish, but instead Muslim. Do Muslims eat turkey? Wouldn't it have to be Halal? Is that even the right word? Or is that what those deep-fried chickpea patties are called? Halals? It sounds almost right.

"No," he says. "Like what happened at the airport five years ago. You know, a real disaster."

Yes. The catastrophe at the airport. Many of your good friends perished that day. Well, not really good friends, but acquaintances with whom you could sustain an involved conversation with for at least ten, if not fifteen, minutes. People whose loss impacted you quite strongly—but not so great as to cause you to mourn them on too-regular of a basis. And generally, you really try to avoid dwelling on those things. "No, I'm sorry to make you think of that. I'm a pilot, actually. That was a terrible day for this city. I was in this very grocery store when it happened. Was buying a chicken salad sandwich, I think it was. Or was it tuna salad?" Now you're uncertain. Just like anyone else, you do enjoy a tuna salad sandwich from time-to-time. But store-made tuna salad is too often overburdened with mayo, creating a gooey, texture-less mess. For some reason chicken salad is usually a little more light on the dressing. "No. I'm pretty sure it was chicken salad."

"Well, I'm sorry to have bothered you. I heard on the radio this morning that the Homeland Security risk level is at red, so I'm kind of on edge. You know?"

No, you don't know how a mere color can put a grown man on edge. You spent more than fifteen years of your life in the Air Force, flying in and out of the most dangerous war zones. You have truly lived a harrowing existence, filled with peril and trauma. But you can't mention this to this stranger. If he is, indeed, a man of the Muslim faith, then there would be a decent probability that you bombed his brethren at some point. He would not appreciate that. "Yeah," you say.

"Anyhow, have a good day. Here's hoping for a white Christmas, right?"

You nod and force out a chuckle, as if your affirmation is obvious. In reality, you hope that the forecast is wrong. Flurries are hardly conducive to reliable and efficient air travel. If that man had a flight to catch on Christmas Day, then surely his tone would be different.

Anyhow, it is time to purchase your items and pick your line. But then you realize that you forgot to grab a pack of wet-wipes. Baby supplies are clear on the other side of the store and you obliviously walked right past them hardly two minutes earlier. Would it be so terrible if you *forgot* to purchase these? Really, you figure that Liam ought to be toilet-trained by now. Shouldn't a three-year-old (who rounds up to four) be able to control his bowels to some reliable degree? You are quite sure that Emma moved on from diapers long before she was his age. In fact, you recall ridiculing other parents (behind their back, of course) who couldn't muster the discipline to properly toilet-train their children. But maybe wet-wipes are part of the problem? Sure, it would be great if every time you wiped your anus you had a soft, warm and lotioned cloth to clean with. But no. You, like all other adults, have to accept that life is inherently difficult. One needs to wipe with arid, harsh paper. Even you—an esteemed pilot working for a mid-sized airline that specializes in short-haul flights across the American Midwest—are not privy to special treatment when nature calls at 36 000 feet. You swab with the same single-ply stuff as those in coach. Barely a step above newsprint. Maybe if you started using airplane-grade toilet paper on your son he'd realize that the jig was up? No more diapers. Time to be a man. Or at least a small boy.

That's it. Ann has been in command of these things for too long. On this matter, you're putting your foot down—no more wet-wipes. You're going to go straight to the checkout. And when you get home you'll pretend that you completely forgot. No need getting into an argument with Ann about this. Just play the absent-minded card. And if she gets snarky, you can always play the Post-Traumatic Stress Disorder card. No one can argue with that.

You approach the idle customers awaiting cashiers, people groaning and looking around as if awaiting their deliverance, and then realize that one of these three lines is actually for the automated self-checkout machines. You've never trusted this technology and remain doubtful that they save any time at all. The man with the turkeys approaches from down the aisle, clearly ready to take his spot in one of the queues. You don't have time to linger. You need to choose now: do you get in one of the lines for a cashier, or do you join the people awaiting an available self-checkout machine?

■ What do you do? ■

Turn to page 10 if you wait in line for one of the cashiers.

Turn to page 73 if you wait for a self-checkout till.

You take your place at the back of the line snaking towards till number eight. The man with the turkeys rolls past you, not even acknowledging your presence (which you think to be a little rude, considering it has not even been thirty seconds since you'd chatted), and stakes his claim at till nine. Poor choice, Turkey Man. Although you don't remember the name of the young employee there, you know him to be one of the slowest workers at this store—struggling to locate barcodes, unsure of how to identify virtually any produce, and bagging each and every item with the slow and deliberate motions of someone rehabilitating from a terrible accident. That said, you have great sympathy for those in physical therapy. Many of your brothers from the military were afflicted with unthinkable injuries in your country's quest to make the world a safer place for all. The first time you saw Carlos after his incident, you almost cried after seeing what had become of him. Almost. Those days of him speeding down the highway in his Jaguar XKR are long gone. But again, you try not to think about these things. Such melancholy contemplations bring you nowhere of use. And, besides, it's not like Carlos decided to seek employment packing bags in a grocery store, did he? Even if that kid did endure a terrible accident in his past, then why would he be put in a frontline situation? Couldn't he stock shelves (preferably after-hours) so as not to get in the way of shoppers? If you are to be upset with anyone, it wouldn't be that kid, but instead the managers of this grocery store. Shouldn't they be aware of this employee's obvious deficiencies? Or perhaps these workers are unionized? If so, it would be yet another example of the antiquated nature of the labor movement. And, yes, you are a member of the Air Line Pilots Association, but that is a union of professionals with legitimate and sought-after skills. Not this.

The line hasn't moved and you make the mistake of checking the time. It's 5:17 in the evening. Ann was assured that you would be home before 5:30, when the first guests were due to arrive. You groan and look behind you. Still the last in line. The man ahead of you has a cart with only a handful of items and has every opportunity to move forward, but instead he remains so focused on the phone in his hand that he doesn't budge. Looking over to till nine, Turkey Man is rolling his own cart forward a few inches. He notices you, granting a quick smile accompanied by a twitching nod of his head. You swear that he's taunting you. And you also figure that he might be of Hispanic descent. It really can be so hard to tell. You look back towards the distracted man ahead of you. There are at least three feet of open space between his cart and the woman ahead. Someone might cut in. Maybe even Turkey Man. You think of telling the customer to move. It's Christmas Eve. People are pressed for time. Get off your darn phone and pay attention to the world around you. You're about to say something.

You clear your throat.

The man chuckles, having read something on his phone. Or perhaps he watched something? You crane your neck to the side to inconspicuously gather a better look at him. He's a Millennial. This is decided because he's younger than you and is not clean shaven. Or does that make him a Hipster? To be honest, you're not really sure of the difference. Didn't they used to be known as Generation Y? Generation Next? Or was that just a Pepsi marketing slogan? If so, well done, Pepsi. But not that it matters. There is now a four-foot gap ahead of his cart and he doesn't move, his eyes so focused on the screen in the palm of his hand. He probably doesn't even care if Turkey Man cuts in. This naive and self-centered Millennial surely doesn't work, likely lives at home, and is spending his parent's money to purchase groceries. He's in no rush. He doesn't have seven different appetizers to prepare (although, really, Ann is doing most of the preparation; you're just laying out the Triscuits, cream cheese, and chili pepper jelly). You have to do something about this. You're the Ace of Spades! You were the best of the best! You've killed people in defense of this great country that isn't so great anymore on account of people like this. If anyone has the right to speak his mind, it's you.

You clear your throat again.

The Millennial turns around, his expression blank, then looks ahead to notice the gap in front of his cart. "Oh, sorry about that." He says to you and rolls the cart forward a few feet.

"Oh," you say as if surprised. "I was just clearing my throat. I wasn't insinuating anything."

He chuckles. "I thought you were giving me a hint."

"No, no, no. It's this dry air. That's all."

"Yeah. I guess it's not like it really matters, does it? It's not like I'm next in line."

"Yeah," you smile and nod. Of course it matters. It's people like him who clog airports. People who stand on the left side of moving sidewalks. People who don't pay attention to their seat numbers when boarding. People who obstruct the corridors while disembarking because they never think that there might be passengers who opt to travel without checked baggage.

He then asks, "You want a lozenge?"

"Sorry?"

"For your throat," he pulls out an opened pack of Halls Cough Drops, the paper wrapping frayed and velvety from handling.

"Uhm," you're dumbfounded by his sudden offer. And shouldn't a hipster such as he be consuming something more artisanal? Craft-made cough drops?

He says, "You mentioned the dry air. I thought it might help." He continues to hold out the pack, the torn edges of paper drooping.

It's the soothing honey lemon flavor, your favorite, but the idea of taking a consumable from a stranger—even if it is wrapped in wax paper—is disgusting. "No thanks. I'm fine."

"Fair enough," he forces the pack back into his pocket. Was that a test? Is he doubting your honesty? He looks forwards again and rolls his cart a couple of inches. If he is testing you, then it doesn't matter, because he seems to have gotten the point.

He then turns back, "They say it might snow tonight."

"Well, I think it's just a chance of flurries."

"Yeah? Someone told me there might be a blizzard."

"I think it was just a fifty-percent chance."

"Well, I hope it snows. It wouldn't be right, it being Christmas and all tomorrow, without snow. Know what I mean?"

You're surprised that this young man even cares, assuming that he will spend the entire holiday on an electronic device. "A white Christmas would look nice. Although, to be honest, I'm not really sure if my daughter would care."

"How old is she?"

"She's nine," you reply and then add, "but going on sixteen, if you know what I mean?"

He pushes out an impassioned laugh. "Yeah."

You are fully aware that he does not know what you mean. How could he? But he glances back towards you and starts inspecting the items in your basket. This shouldn't bother you (since you'd already analyzed the contents of his cart), but he does so with such flagrance that it is unsettling. Is he studying your groceries in hope of coming up with a new topic of conversation? Why would he care? Just a minute ago, he was so engrossed in his phone that he didn't realize that there was a gaping chasm in front of him. He looks back up to you, ready to say something, then sighs and glances back towards the front of the line.

Now you feel pressured to chat. At least he made an attempt at small-talk, commenting on the weather and asking about your daughter. He even offered you a soothing honey lemon Halls Cough Drop. It is clear that he has been the better person here—the

Millennial! He looks towards the line at the adjacent till (where Turkey Man has definitely moved ahead of you) and then back towards your basket. The last thing he asked you was about the age of your daughter.

You say, "I also have a son. He's three."

He seems surprised by your sudden admission, as if now uneasy with your desire to continue talking. "Oh yeah." He turns back, pushes his cart ahead another foot, and takes out his phone. Within seconds, he's typing something with furiously nimble thumbs. Is he writing about you? Is he tweeting about this awkward middle-aged man in a grocery store? If only he knew about the things you've done in your old life. The adventure. The sex. The death. He probably thinks you're just a bank teller. Or a teacher. Perhaps you should continue to wear your military uniform? People treated you differently then. But you also know that it wouldn't fit. You must have gained at least thirty pounds since you've left the Air Force. A uniform demands respect—yes—but the effect is lessened when each button strains with all its might to keep each side together.

The line moves and the Millennial starts placing his groceries onto the conveyor. Things are happening. Once again, you're ahead of Turkey Man. And say what you will about Millennials, but this one knows the drill. He has his supermarket club card out before the cashier can ask and places his credit card on the counter, ready to make quick-work of his payment. He then pulls up his cart to grant you space to place your groceries. And right as you put down your first item—the plastic tub of Philadelphia cream cheese—you hear the introductory, spaced-out-synth notes of *Wonderful Christmastime* playing over the store's unseen speakers. This feels like a good omen. Although not necessarily your favorite Beatles song (to be honest, you find most of their compositions a little too boring for your liking), this is definitely one of your favorite Christmas tunes. You start humming along, remembering that time Carlos told you that it wasn't actually a Beatles song. This was before the age of smartphones and you didn't have the opportunity to prove him wrong. Before any further thoughts of Carlos' misfortune can return to your thoughts, you quietly sing/hum while placing your groceries:

"The mood is right, the spirit's up.

We're here tonight, and that's enough.

Simply having, a wonderful—"

"Sorry," the cashier says to you. "I'm going to have to cash out."

The Millennial places his bags into the cart and rolls away, giving you a nod and lazy wave, his parting gift.

"What's that?" You say to the cashier.

"I have to leave early." She's withdrawn her entire tray of cash and coins. "My colleague is on her way right now to fill in. It'll just be a sec."

"But I've only got eight items."

"Sorry, but I've already logged out. Don't worry. I think I can see her right now." She shrugs and takes her tray with her, leaving you alone with your groceries. Looking behind you, there is now just one other person in line, a haggard looking man with wispy, thinning blond hair carrying nothing but a single, unwieldy box of diapers. Size two. His child mustn't be even six months old.

He notices that there is no one at the till and reacts with a dramatic sigh before asking, "What's going on?"

"It's a shift change, I guess. The lady said that someone else would be on shortly. Although, I don't see anyone coming."

The man shakes his head. "Great," he moans sarcastically.

You nod in sympathy—although, really, you wonder just why this guy doesn't go to one of the self-checkout machines? Perhaps, in some parallel universe, you did decide to go into the self-checkout line. Well, then in this alternate reality you are surely living a far more fulfilling and time-efficient life than this. Turkey Man has just finished heaving each of his frozen beasts onto the conveyor of the adjacent till and is partaking in small-talk with the cashier. You stretch your neck in an attempt to locate this replacement employee, but see no one approaching from any direction. "This is ridiculous," you mutter.

"A disaster," the man with the diapers adds.

Yes, you think. A disaster. Feeling a tepid kinship with this man because of his use of hyperbole, you then ask, "How old is your kid?"

"Five months," he says with a sigh. "But they say it gets easier after the first six months, right?"

"Yeah," you say, as if that was true. It's not.

"You have any kids?" he asks.

"Yeah. Two. Boy and a girl."

"How old?"

"The girl is nine—but she's going on sixteen, if you know what I mean?"

Diaper Man forces out a weak chuckle.

You then add, "And my boy is just three."

"Ah, so you must be out of this stage, right?" He holds up his box of diapers.

Size two? What kind of pigmy offspring does this follicly-challenged man think you have produced? You're essentially six feet in height! (Actually, you are five feet and nine inches.) You resist the urge to snicker. "Yes, we're well past size two."

"No, I mean, just diapers, in general. You must be done with diapers, then. Right?"

"Oh. Yes."

He clearly senses your trepidation. "Oh, no, sorry. I mean, if you're not, that's totally normal."

"Nothing to apologize about." He should be sorry. What makes this man such an authority on the topic? He clearly has but a single child. However, you cannot backtrack now. "My boy has been toilet trained for years."

He's taken aback. "For *years*? When did you start toilet training him?"

"Well, I have to say that you really can't start early enough."

"So, before he was one?"

You said years. Plural. Why did you do that? But you are a proud man. And proud men do not admit to mistakes or lies. Proud men repeat their lies with such conviction that it becomes the truth. "I'd say we started when he was ten months old."

"Wow."

"Well, I was in the military. I know a thing or two about the importance of discipline."

"Any hot tips?"

"Uh," again, you look around for the cashier, really wishing he or she (most likely a she) would be approaching at that second. Still no one. "I would recommend against using wet-wipes."

"Really? Why's that?"

"Too coddling. Makes them enjoy the entire process."

"Huh. I've never heard that one before."

"Take it from me. I know."

"You just use regular toilet paper?"

"Well, two-ply. I'm not a savage."

"Of course." Diaper Man is impressed and you're glad to have passed on such wisdom to another person. Even if it is entirely unfounded. He adds, "I tell you, if Santa was real, all I'd ask for is an end to these darn diapers."

Although you chuckle, you wonder what a grown man is doing talking about *if Santa was real*, even if it is all in jest? Is he one of those guys who speaks of going to the *little boys room*? You want to shake him. Tell him to be a man.

"Okay," Diaper Man says, shaking his head. "This is ridiculous. We shouldn't be waiting this long. I'm going to the self-checkouts."

You also think of doing the exact same thing, but that would entail retrieving your basket (which is tucked at the top of an orderly stack beneath the counter) and placing all eight of your items back within it. And then—only then—would you find yourself *behind* Diaper Man in line.

But the very next moment you see movement from down the corridor. A uniform-clad woman is walking towards your till with a fresh tray for the register. Maybe Diaper Man wasn't so wise? Maybe you were right to hold your ground?

No. All your enthusiasm drains away like a punctured can of 7-Up. It's not just any cashier. It's Taryl. Everything with her seems to take forever, terminating any chances you may have had to get out of this supermarket in a prompt manner. "Hey, you," she says with a cheerful smile as if you two are friends, although she clearly can't remember your name (to be fair, you only know hers because of the tag on her lapel). "Doing some last minute Christmas shopping?" she asks while attempting to slide in her tray of coins and bills. It takes a couple of hearty pushes, but it then glides in and she is able to close the drawer.

"Just picking up a few things for our annual Christmas Eve appie party."

"Oh, that sounds nice."

"Yeah," you say, "We've been doing this for more than ten years now."

"That sounds great."

"It is." Contrary to what you assure to Taryl, you would never describe your annual Christmas Eve appie-party as being *great*. It's pretty-good. It's enjoyable. It's pleasurable. The best part will be partaking in several liberal ladles of Ann's famous holiday punch that will be sitting prominently in the middle of the kitchen island. The inclusion of Cranberry 7-Up to the recipe will really make for a fun, festive cocktail. With any luck, you'll abide in several of these, everyone will leave before eleven o'clock, and you'll be able to enjoy a hassle-free and only mildly inebriated slumber straight through until seven in the morning, ensuring a solid eight hours of sleep.

Taryl uses the corner of her employee card to punch in various unseen codes onto the screen. You've seen many of her kind doing this exact same thing: tapping the screen with a card instead of just using their fingers. Is this a hygiene thing? If so, shouldn't she just wear latex gloves? You've seen some cashiers do this, and it makes great sense, considering the filthy nature of physical currency.

"Excuse me?" You ask.

"What's that?"

"I was actually wondering why it is that you use your card to type things into the screen instead of just using your fingers?"

"Oh," she pulls back the card, which dangles from a lanyard around her neck. "I don't know. Everyone does it."

"But do you know why?"

"Never really thought about it. It's just what you do. Maybe cause it looks kinda cool?"

Does it? Does it look cool? A man in a pilot's uniform, fabric smooth and taut, the short-brim of his hat gleaming beneath the fluorescent glow of an airport's waiting lounge—that looks cool. Hitting a touch-activated screen with the rounded corner of a plastic card—not cool. You neglect to share these thoughts with Taryl, however, instead opting for a placid, "Yeah."

"Okay, then." She asks, "Do you have your customer club card?"

Do you look like someone who enjoys needlessly paying more for goods? "Of course," you pass it over and she scans the card.

"Thanks," she replies and hands it back. She then grabs the loaf of bread and swipes it through the scanner, eliciting a single chirp from the machine, and places it at the bottom of a plastic bag. You immediately fear that she is going to ruin that delectably soft flaxseed loaf by smothering it with your remaining items. Those potatoes alone must weigh more than a couple of pounds.

"Oh," she then says, realizing a mistake. "I forgot to ask, did you even need a bag?"

What did she think you were going to do? Carry all these items out between your folded arms? "Yes, please."

"I mean, I wasn't sure if you had your own. You know, one of those reusable ones?"

"Yeah. My wife always makes sure that she brings one."

Taryl looks up and behind you. "Oh, does she have one?"

"No, she's not here."

"And you don't have one?"

"No."

"Oh." She seems almost shocked, disappointed. "Okay." She puts the bread back into the bottom of the plastic bag. She then grabs the jar of chili pepper jelly and swipes it through. You watch her hand as it vanishes behind the drooping lip of the plastic bag.

"Wait!"

"What?"

"Shouldn't you put the bread on top of other items?"

Taryl laughs and then shakes her head. "Don't worry. I have space at the bottom. I'm putting these things around the bread. I would never put something heavy on top of a loaf of bread like that. This isn't my first rodeo, you know?"

"Oh, sorry." You say, although you feel absolutely no sense of culpability here. In fact, you wonder if that laugh of hers was really more of a scoff. The distinction between the two is far too blurry a line for your liking.

She then retrieves the glass jar of jelly and reads the label. "Is this, like, spicy jam?"

"I guess that's a good way to put it."

"You put it on your toast?"

You laugh (actually, it is more of a scoff). "I put it out with the hors d'oeuvres."

"Sorry?"

"It's really good on a cracker topped with cream cheese."

"Huh." She then notices the tub of Philadelphia cream cheese. "I guess that explains this then, right?" She swipes it through with her other hand and blindly places the container into the bag. But her eyes continue to focus on the jar of jelly. "Is it kinda sweet?"

"I guess, a little."

She then turns to inspect the other side of the label. "Oh yeah."

Although not keen on the idea of a cashier thoroughly inspecting the details of your groceries, you ask: "What's that?"

"Sugar is the first ingredient."

"Really?"

"Yeah. So I guess it really must be sweet."

"It is a jelly."

"Well, *'Tis the season*, right?" she says.

"For spicy food?"

"For sweet things."

"Oh. Yes."

Something seems to grab her attention and she pauses. She then places the jar into the bag without looking and glances back to you. "You know what I bet that jam would be really good with?"

"What's that?"

"A turkey sandwich."

You are repulsed and surely your expression hides nothing. "Why?"

"Hear me out. It's sweet, like cranberry sauce, and who doesn't love cranberry sauce with their turkey? And it's spicy. And I like a little bit of kick on my sandwich."

"I don't like a little bit of kick on my sandwich."

"Really?" She cocks her head while inspecting you. "You

always struck me as someone who likes a little heat."

"What do you mean by that?"

"I don't know. You're a guy. I always assume guys like things a little spicy."

Interesting generalization. You decide to investigate this further, starting with a mental list of the male adults in your life with whom you're close enough with to be able to ascertain their penchant for spice. The first person you think of is Carlos, and, yes, he likes his food *picante*, as they say. Or is it *caliente?* However, this also seems invalid because of his Latin-American descent. It's a given, isn't it? Wouldn't Latino women also have an increased tolerance for spice? You think of your neighbor, Roger Wang, but you can't remember ever taking note of what his tolerance for spice would be. While the man continues to lay claim to the most luscious lawn on your block, he cannot also claim the crown as the most extroverted in your neighborhood. In the six years you two have lived adjacent to one another, he's hardly ever made an effort to have an involved conversation with you. As a newcomer to this country, one would think that he would want to immerse himself in his adopted culture? Granted, you're not actually sure if he was born in China. You've never asked him where he was from. You've never really asked him anything. Just the occasional thumbs up or congenial nod.

"What are you thinking about?" Taryl asks, at which point you realize that she has yet to scan another item.

"Just about your comment regarding men liking spicy food more than women."

"And you know what's interesting?"

"What's that?"

"I've never thought about this before, but Christmas food and spice really don't go together."

"Well, our family does have quite the penchant for chili pepper jelly with cream cheese on crackers."

"True, but that's not really a tried-and-true Christmas favorite, is it?

"I think it is."

"Yeah, but I'm not sure if the average person would feel the same way."

"I don't think it's that unusual."

Taryl then reaches for the corded phone at her till. "Why don't I call Misty, my supervisor? See what she thinks?"

"I don't think that's really necessary."

She shrugs, indifferent to the matter, and leaves the phone. She seems to have forgotten just what she's supposed to be doing (i.e. scanning and bagging the remaining groceries). "Can you think of anything else?"

"What's that?"

"Spicy foods at Christmas? Or maybe I should say *during The Holidays?*"

"I don't mind if you say Christmas."

"What about Jewish food? Is it spicy?"

"I don't think so."

"You don't have any Jewish friends?"

"Well, of course." You say, almost as if insulted. You're about to say that you have *many* friends who follow the Jewish faith, but that would seem to be a bit much. You live in the American Midwest, after all. "I just don't really know much about their eating habits."

"I don't think their food is spicy."

"I'm not really sure. Judaism is from The Middle East. There is quite a lot of spice in those cuisines."

"I guess Israel is in The Middle East, isn't it? I always think of it being, I don't know, less far away. More, like, European. You know what I mean?"

This young woman's appreciation for world geography is

appalling. As a pilot who has literally flown around the world on numerous occasions, you find this inexcusable. That said, you decide against making your disappointment known. "I guess."

"But you still can't think of any other spicy holiday foods, can you?"

"I guess not."

Taryl chuckles and then shrugs her shoulders before returning to her job. She takes the box of Triscuits, scans it through, and then places it in the bag. "Those must be for the cream cheese and spicy jam appie?"

"Yup."

She scans through the bag of rolled oats. "What are these for?"

You begin, "Well—"

"Actually," she interrupts, noticing the next item on the conveyor: a bag of Sun-Maid Raisins. "Let me guess. You're making oatmeal-raisin cookies?"

Impressive. Giving credit where credit is due, you heartily nod. "The kids do love them."

She scans the raisins and then stops to ask, "How old are your kids again?"

"My son is three. And my daughter is nine. But going on sixteen, if you know what I mean?"

"Yeah," she chuckles with a knowing nod. "My niece is four."

You're not sure what her niece being four years of age would have to do with appreciating the pre-adolescent tendencies of your daughter, but you let it go. Or, perhaps her four-year-old niece is already behaving like a diva, in which case you would hate to think to what degree that child has been pampered in her short life. You ask, "She must be pretty excited about tomorrow?"

"Oh, yeah. She's all about Christmas these days."

"You see her a lot?"

"No. She lives in Miami. But, you know."

"Yeah."

"How about your boy? You said he was four, right?"

"No, he's three."

"Ah, same difference, right?"

"Well, a year."

"Yeah, well, he must be all revved up, right?"

"He is pretty excited."

"What's Santa bringing him this year?"

You're annoyed with this question for three reasons. First, while Taryl asks and then waits, she once again neglects her employee obligations. Second, you find it almost patronizing that she asks you what "*Santa is bringing,*" as if Liam is in your vicinity and there is a pressing need to keep up with the big lie about the existence of Santa Claus. But third (and most importantly), you can't remember anything in particular that Liam is receiving for Christmas. Ann does all the shopping. "Oh, you know, lots of stuff."

"There must be one thing that he's really excited about?"

Why does she keep pressing you on this matter? Can she tell that you don't know? And if so, is she judging you to be a terrible parent? Personally, you feel that Liam is spoiled enough as it is on a day-to-day basis and whatever extra gifts he'll be getting are just superfluous. Perhaps if the boy had to earn a little more of what he's had bestowed upon him then you'd have some leverage in this whole toilet-training thing? And yet Taryl continues to stare at you expectantly, awaiting an answer.

You answer: "A ball."

"A ball?"

"Yes. A ball. He's really excited about getting a ball."

"He doesn't already have one?"

He has dozens. "He has a few."

"What kind of ball?"

"What do you mean?"

"Like a basketball? Or a baseball? Or a soccer ball?"

Definitely not a soccer ball. Does she not know that you're a born-and-bred American? "A football."

"Huh. Is it from his favorite team?"

"Yes."

"Cool." She runs the raisins through the scanner and puts them into the bag.

"Oh, excuse me?" you say.

"What's that?"

"I think you ran those through already."

"Did I?" she asks.

Of course she did. You can see it right on the digital display. She looks at the screen and then confirms that there is not another pack already in the bag. "Oh shoot. I'm sorry. Not very Christmas-like of me, was that?"

"That's okay. Mistakes happen." Of course, in your profession, customers have absolutely zero tolerance for any and all errors. It seems that Taryl is in the appropriate line of work.

"I'll just cancel that last one." She pulls out her employee identification card and taps the screen with it. She then pauses and her expression contorts while her hands remain idle.

You ask, "Is everything okay?"

"It's not cancelling."

"Is it frozen?"

She taps the screen three times in a row with her card. "No. It's just not letting me cancel." She reaches towards the phone again. "I can call my manager if you want."

You really don't want to go down that path. All you have left are the potatoes and the limited edition Cranberry 7-Up. "Can't you try again?"

"If it's not working now, I'm not sure what trying again would do. But, okay." She bangs the screen repeatedly with her index finger. "I don't get it. It's just not letting me cancel. But, if you want to speed this up, why don't you just go pick up another bag of raisins on your way out and then I don't have to cancel anything?"

What initially seems to be an absurd notion swiftly sounds intriguing. You love genuine California raisins. And no matter how many you have in your house, you doubt that they will expire. The dehydrating process is inherently one of preservation.

"So, what do you think?" Taryl asks.

You're not sure. You don't want to take too long and worry about delaying the other busy shoppers. Looking behind you, there is only one person behind you in line, a middle-aged woman of some sort of east-Asian descent. Ten years ago, you would have used the word *Oriental* to describe her, but have since learned that the term is not politically correct. You're not sure if it's actually derogatory or just out-of-style. Come to think of it, you're quite certain it can't actually be too harsh or demeaning, considering that you can still purchase the *Oriental appetizer party pack* from the frozen food section of this very grocery store. These delectable variety samplers include spring rolls, something crescent shaped, something triangle shaped, and something in a crispy golden cup (as well as several packs of plum sauce). Just arrange these items (still frozen) on a cookie sheet and place them in the oven for 10-12 minutes at 350 degrees Fahrenheit, and what emerges is a guaranteed hit. Your mouth is watering just thinking of how delicious any one of these would taste right now.

It's decided then. You're going to get that second pack of raisins and also pick up an Oriental appetizer party pack. Although quite certain that Ann will not be impressed with your executive decision to purchase this addition to your annual Christmas Eve appie party, you figure it doesn't matter. It's Christmas. People can have what they want.

"All right then," you say. "I think I'm going to get the second pack of raisins."

"Great!" Taryl says with an unusual degree of enthusiasm.

"Should I go right now to pick it up?"

"Why don't I just ring through these last couple things first, then you can pay up and get the raisins on the way out?"

Although Taryl's plan is quite prudent for the situation that she is aware of, it does not take into account your newfound desire for the Oriental appetizer party pack. "I was actually thinking of picking up one more thing while I was at it."

"Oh, what was that?"

You glance towards the elderly east-Asian woman just behind you and then back to Taryl. "It's one of those frozen appetizer packs."

"Those always are a hit when it comes to dinner parties, aren't they?"

"They certainly are."

"Which one?"

"It has a few different things."

"What's it called?"

"I can't remember the exact name."

"What was in it?"

"Like, spring rolls. And a few other things."

"Like Chinese food stuff?"

"I don't know if all the items are based on cuisines from the country of China, so much, as the general region of that part of the world."

"I think I know which one you're talking about." Taryl reaches for the phone. "I'll just call someone and ask them to pick it up."

"No, no, I can just get it."

"Was it the Oriental appetizer party pack?" she asks.

You need to resist any temptation to see if the woman behind you is listening. With any luck, her English skills are so poor that she is entirely unaware of this conversation. "That might be it."

"That is a good one. It was on special a couple of weeks ago. Buy-one-get-one-free."

You love a BOGO. Especially a quality BOGOF, which is all too rare. "Do you know if it is still on sale?"

"I don't think so. Do you remember what it cost? I could just ring it through as general grocery and then you could pick it up with the raisins."

"No, I just thought of it while I was in line."

"Because of the Oriental woman behind you?"

You turn back, feign a reaction of disturbed shock, shake your head and return your focus to Taryl. "No. Not at all. And I don't believe people use that term anymore."

"Well, they must if it's the name of the product, right?"

You look back towards the perhaps-Chinese lady, who thankfully still seems oblivious to what has been taking place ahead of her in line. You then notice that she has but a single item—a one-quart jug of buttermilk, which she cradles tightly between her arms as if someone might try to pry it away at any moment. You are still scarred (metaphorically, of course) by that time you unwittingly poured buttermilk into your coffee (another disaster) and wonder if this woman has picked up the wrong dairy product. Do they even have buttermilk in Asia? And frankly, what *is* buttermilk? How can a man in his mid-forties not know what buttermilk is and yet still find it in his fridge on a semi-regular basis? Should you say something to this woman?

"Are you going to ask her if it's a bad word?" Taryl asks.

"What? No. I was just. Never mind."

"So, what do you want to do about that *other* item?" She accompanies her vague adjective with a wink, as if to imply that you two are somehow on the same team.

"I guess I really should decide quickly."

"You wouldn't happen to know the UPC, would you? Then I could just type it in right here and find the price."

"The U-P, what?"

"UPC? It's the twelve number code on all items."

"Oh, the one right by the barcode?"

"Yeah."

"Does anyone know such a code for things they buy? I didn't even know the price."

Taryl shrugs. "I know it for certain things."

"Like what?"

"Well, it's zero-three-eight-zero-zero-zero-five-seven-six-zero-eight-nine for Kellogg's Cornflakes."

You're impressed. In an age where Millennials don't even have to memorize seven digit phone numbers, the fact that this seemingly simple woman is able to rattle off the entire code so effortlessly leaves you a little more optimistic about this new generation. Unless, of course, she just made that up.

She then says, "You don't believe me, do you?"

"Not at all."

"I can see it in your face. I don't blame you. I could have just made that up. Here, let me prove it." She taps a couple of points on the screen and then rapidly pecks away, inputting each of the twelve digits with a clattering tap from her nails. A moment later, the customer display is updated with: *Kellogg's Cornflakes. 26.8 oz. $2.89.*

You say, "I never doubted you, but still I have to admit that I'm impressed."

"Thanks."

"Now just let me—oh, shoot."

"What's that?"

"I was going to cancel the item. But I can't. You know? Like the whole raisin thing."

You can't help but groan, turning back towards the perhaps-

Japanese woman and muttering an apology, to which she nods quickly, as if giving you permission to carry on.

Taryl adds: "Sorry about that. It is a pretty good price, though. If you want, you could just pick it up, along with the raisins and the Oriental appetizer party pack."

This is ridiculous. It's Christmas Eve, you are already late, Ann will surely call you at any time to voice her displeasure, and now this. You should have been back in your Volvo sedan ages ago. Well, not ages. Minutes. Perhaps eight. Looking at the self-checkout, you don't recognize anyone. Not even Diaper Man. They've all moved on. This is truly a disaster.

And yet, at the same time, Taryl is right. $2.89 for a package of brand-name cereal is an impressive bargain. Even if you still have a box brimming full of corn flakes back at home, what could be the drawback of purchasing another? As long as the bag within is not punctured, the cereal would remain flaky and crispy until the time came to enjoy them.

Heck, even if you already have several boxes at home, then you'll simply put an extra scoop into your bowl each morning. There is no downside to this. Clearly, Taryl is able to read your blossoming expression and she says: "You're going to get it, aren't you?"

"I do love Kellogg's corn flakes."

"Should we do this then?"

"I think so." You are tempted to raise your hand to high-five Taryl, but that would be a little over the top. Instead, you tap one hand on the counter a couple of times. "I'll pick it up when I get the raisins."

"And the Oriental appetizer party pack."

"Well, I'm not sure—"

"Oh, I assumed that you were going through with that. And all this talk about Orientals is making me want to pick up a pack before I go home today. Hey, and you know what's interesting?" She then awaits your reply. How is there any way you can possibly know what she is about to talk about?

"No. What?"

"Guess what the main ingredient in plum sauce is?"

You want to say *plums*, but that is too obvious and definitely would not warrant Taryl's interjection. "I don't know."

"Ah, you have to make at least one guess."

Fair enough. You don't enjoy it when other people try to get away from such queries without divulging even a single response. "Maybe sugar?"

"Pumpkins."

"Really?"

"Yeah. Should be called pumpkin sauce."

Taryl is right. That was interesting. If it's true. You'll need to confirm the validity of her statement at a later time (hopefully when you grab a box of the Oriental appetizer party pack). You then ask, "Did we ever figure out how much they cost? I can't remember. It feels like I've been here forever." Glancing back towards the perhaps-Korean lady, you grimace and add, "Sorry. I'm almost done."

She nods quickly, her eyes stoic and without concern.

"You know," Taryl smiles, "I've got an idea. It is Christmas Eve, and all."

"What's that?"

"Why don't I just ring in a *general grocery* item for, I don't know, how about two-ninety-nine? Then you can just pick it up on the way out with the raisins and the corn flakes."

Honestly, you were hoping that she was going to tell you to just take it for free, or "*On the house*," as they say in bars. Which gets you thinking: why isn't that phrase used within the context of a grocery store? "*Buy one, get one 'on the house?*' " A BOGOOTH. It sounds rather cool.

"Well?" Taryl asks.

"Sure. That sounds great."

"'Tis the season, right?"

You're not sure what she means by that, but you smile and agree with a breathy chuckle. She places the bag of potatoes on the scale and searches the transparent plastic for some sort of tag or marking. "Do you know what type of potatoes these are?"

"I don't know. Aren't they just potatoes?"

"Well, there are different types."

"Maybe brown ones?"

"That's not an option." She starts reading the screen to you: "There are russet potatoes, white potatoes, red potatoes, yellow potatoes, mini-red potatoes, mini-yellow potatoes, red table potatoes, nugget potatoes, fingerling potatoes, white potatoes. Did I say white potatoes already?"

"I think you did."

"And that doesn't even include all the organic potatoes." She looks back to the screen. You are about to tell her that there's no reason for her to read all these aloud (even though Ann continues to purchase organic produce, you refuse to do so when alone), but there is no stopping her. "Organic russet. Organic white. Organic red. Organic mini-red Organic nugget." She then huffs. "That's interesting."

"What's that?"

"There are no organic yellow potatoes."

"That is interesting."

"Yeah. Wonder why?"

"Maybe just out of stock?"

"No. This tells me if it's out of stock. We just don't carry them."

"Huh. Strange."

"And all of that doesn't even include the sweet potatoes or

yams."

"You probably would have a few different varieties of those, wouldn't you?"

"I could read them out, if you think that might be what you bought."

"No, I'm certain I didn't get sweet potatoes or yams."

"You sure? I mean, not to be rude, but you said you didn't know what type of potato you purchased."

"Fair enough. But I know it's not a yam."

"How so?"

"Yams are more of an orangey color."

"True that."

"And I would assume sweet potatoes would be in a different section. I just got these with all the other potatoes."

Taryl nods, looks at the bag and then back to the screen. You assume that she should be able to discern the difference, considering that this is her job. If asked to distinguish between a stratus, stratocumulus, cumulonimbus, or cirrus cloud, you'd find this task so easy that you could accomplish it with your eyes closed. Well, obviously not literally. But figuratively.

"How about russet?" you advise.

"That sounds good." She taps the screen and the subtotal appears. "Plus, russets seem to be the cheapest ones, so why not, right?"

You're not sure how to take this. Does this career-stagnant woman think that you can only afford the least-expensive potatoes to bring home to your family? Or does she think you told her to ring them in as russet because they had the lowest cost per pound? Either way, this seems a little insulting. You served your country in several armed conflicts. What has she ever done?

"Are you okay?" she asks while sliding over your last item on the conveyor, the limited edition 12-pack of Cranberry 7-Up.

"Oh, yeah. I'm fine."

"Hmm. This looks interesting. Cranberry 7-Up? I've never seen this before."

"It's new. I believe it's only around for a short time."

"Have you tried it before?"

"No, but it sounds delicious. Nothing says *The Holidays* like a cranberry, I'd say."

Taryl thinks about this. "I'm going to have to agree to disagree with you on that one. Personally, I think a candy-cane really sums up this time of year. I mean, do you ever eat candy canes at any other time?"

Honestly, you don't eat candy canes at *any* time of the year. But she does make a good point. The chances of you being able to purchase a box of candy canes in August would be highly unlikely, whereas a bag of Ocean Spray cranberries can be found throughout the year. Or is that only the frozen variety? Either way, people have the option of enjoying cranberry sauce even in the off-season. Candy canes, not so much. "You are right. Although, I don't think the peppermint taste of a candy cane would really go with 7-Up."

"Oh, no. It would be like drinking soda right after brushing your teeth."

"Exactly."

She scans the box and lifts it towards your bag of goods. For a moment, she seems to contemplate finding a way to force the entire item into the crammed bag. She then shakes her head, pulls up the plastic bag with your groceries, places it on the adjacent counter, and puts the pack of 7-Up into its very own, otherwise empty bag.

"Oh, you don't need to put that in a bag."

"Did I forget to ask you if you had your own?"

"No, you asked. I told you that my wife usually brings a few, but I always forget."

"She's the more environmentally inclined one, right?"

"I don't know if I said that. But I didn't bring a bag."

"Okay then." Taryl appears confused, holding the pack of Cranberry 7-Up in the air, unsure what to do with it. "So, where do you want this, then?"

"I can just carry it on its own."

"Oh, I see." She then puts it down beside your bag of groceries. "Just like that?"

"That's great."

"You're not walking far, are you?"

You can't withhold a scoff. Does she actually think that you walked here? What kind of well-heeled man carries bags of groceries any farther than the distance from a checkout to his car? "No. I have a really close parking spot, actually."

"Because if it was a long way, then I could double-bag your groceries."

Now you're unsure. Either the structural integrity of the plastic is so poor that it can't reliably handle even a small number of groceries, or—and this is the worst-case scenario—Taryl overloaded so many groceries into a single bag that no reasonable person would expect the plastic to survive the short journey. And your bread! With the flax seeds! Is it not right at the bottom, beneath everything else? What sorry state must that once-luscious loaf now be in, straddled by potatoes, oatmeal and raisins? And to think that she was going to try to force that 12-pack of Cranberry 7-Up into the mix!

This might just end up being the worst Christmas Eve ever.

Okay. The worst Christmas Eve ever would most definitely be the one you spent in Afghanistan in the winter of 2002. Never before had you felt so cold—physically, spiritually, emotionally. After the horrors that you'd witnessed, you felt the very purpose in your life drain away, leaving your world washed-out, without meaning, without love. You were forced to confront the very core of your being, of what it meant to be a soldier, an American, a human.

And still now, you do not know what answers you found, what solace you'd gleaned. Ann never knew what you'd endured while you were away, while you spent the Christmas season on the other side of the world, your very soul as vacant as an empty can of 7-Up discarded on the side of the Interstate.

So, that would make this the second-worst Christmas Eve ever.

You then look back to the elderly perhaps-Vietnamese woman behind you, still waiting patiently while clasping her single quart of buttermilk, seemingly unbothered by the absurd amount of time it is taking for you to scan through your groceries. How is she not annoyed? Is this a cultural thing? Is her static expression a mere facade hiding her inner rage? Is this how lines progress in Vietnam? Or is she just so darn appreciative to be in the greatest country in the world that even a grocery store lineup on Christmas Eve is something to savor? You nod, realizing that even though you have forty-five years of life experience behind you, even though you've travelled the world and seen things that most men couldn't fathom, you still have things to learn.

Taryl says, "So, that's a yes?"

"To what, again?"

She lifts up the burdened bag of groceries and slips it into a second. "I double-bagged it. I saw you nodding."

"Oh. Sure."

"So," she taps the screen and absorbs the total, "that will be fifty-eight seventy. But, I thought I should let you know that we have a promotion right now. If you spend a bit more you can get a free frozen turkey. It's like a twenty-dollar value, free of charge."

Even though Ann already purchased a turkey and there is no pressing need for additional poultry in your house, you are intrigued. "How much more?"

"About a hundred dollars."

"What?"

"You have to spend over one-hundred-and-fifty dollars to receive the free turkey."

"That's not a little bit more."

"I think I just said, *a bit more.*"

"That's a lot more to spend."

"It's a really good deal."

"If I didn't have to spend another hundred dollars."

"Well, I thought I'd offer." She looks over both shoulders and then leans in. "Management is really pushing the deal. I kinda figured I should ask."

"Fair enough," you say, appreciative of the need to follow the commands of your superiors. "But, to be honest, don't you think it's a bit late to be offering turkeys to people? I mean, it's Christmas tomorrow. If someone is going to have a turkey dinner, they'd surely have already procured the main course."

"That's a good point. We should probably make it more like, spend sixty-five bucks, get a free turkey."

Now that would be a deal you'd partake in. All you'd have to spend would be an additional six dollars and thirty cents. Looking around the immediate vicinity of impulse-purchase-worthy items, you'd just have to get a few packs of gum, maybe a couple of chocolate bars (at least one 3 Musketeers, of course), and some Tic Tacs. But would you really need that much junk food? The sad truth is that the first thing you would do upon stepping foot into the parking lot is retrieve one of those chocolate bars (most definitely the 3 Musketeers), rip apart the flimsy packaging and tear into the milk chocolate and delectable whipped nougat.

You pretend to scratch a sudden itch just above your belt, when really you survey the burgeoning mass of middle-aged fat that surrounds your waist. Your midsection has become a perverse version of that 3 Musketeers bar: a thin outer layer holding back a great mass of whipped nougat. Yes, turkey is a healthy, lean meat, but any potential health benefits of consuming more of it in the coming weeks would be greatly outweighed by the increased confectionary consumption.

No, even if all you needed to do was spend a total of sixty-five dollars to be rewarded a free frozen turkey (itself, up to a twenty dollar value!), you would turn down the offer. At some point in a man's life, he has to take a stand. He has to say, "*Enough!*" It's time to start jogging again. It's time to dust off that Bowflex Max Trainer in the garage. It's time to cut back on the sweets, on the chicken wings... even on the 7-Up. Or, at least drink the sugar-free variety— although Ann refuses to allow anything containing aspartame in your house, claiming the sweetener causes a great assortment of ailments and should not be within reach of your children. You'd have to keep the Diet 7-Up out of sight, perhaps in the garage somewhere, maybe even behind the Bowflex Max Trainer. It's ridiculous that you'll have to start hiding diet sodas in your own house, as if you were some sort of shameful addict, but this might be the only way forward. You then look at the box of Cranberry 7-Up on the counter in front of you, wondering if you should replace it with the diet option. Was there even a diet variety? You can't remember.

But then you think: It's the holiday season. It's a time for being a little naughty. You'll begin concealing cans of Diet 7-Up after New Year's Day.

Taryl is leaning against the register while texting on her phone with a subtle, twitching smile. Looking over to the perhaps-Malaysian woman, who continues to wait her turn while neither you nor Taryl says a word, you decide to get the cashier's attention. "Excuse me," you say.

"Oh, hey. Sorry." She types for a few more seconds, sends the message, and puts the phone back into her pocket. "Did you make a decision about the free turkey?"

"Am I able to get one if I spend sixty-five dollars?"

Taryl snorts. "Oh no, I don't have the authority to allow a deal like that. You'd have to spend over a hundred and fifty."

"Then, no."

"You know, can I tell you something kinda crazy?" Taryl says while leaning forward.

"What's that?"

"I don't even like turkey."

That *is* crazy. "Not even with gravy?"

Taryl just shrugs. "Yeah, it's better with gravy—"

"—Of course."

"Yeah, of course. But I just find it, kinda, well, boring."

"Wait a minute. You just told me that you thought that chili pepper jelly would go great on a turkey sandwich."

"Oh, I like turkey on a sandwich. I mean, that's all about all the other things on it. But on its own, it's just." She shrugs again. "Blah."

You didn't think this was possible. Looking over to the perhaps-Thai woman, you figure that she would enjoy a steaming turkey dinner, even if she'd never before enjoyed one. The tastes and textures seem as universally appealing as a glass of sweet and sparkling 7-Up soda. "Did you like it as a kid?"

"It was okay." Again, she reacts with that indifferent shrug. It almost makes you angry. "It wasn't something I liked as much as pizza or spaghetti."

"So, what are you going to have for Christmas dinner tomorrow?"

"My folks usually make a ham these days."

You struggle to repress your reaction, an emotion right on the knife's edge between surprise and repulsion. "On Christmas Day?"

"Yeah. Why not?"

"That's an Easter meal."

"Why can't it be a Christmas meal?"

Now, it should be stated that you enjoy a succulent and juicy honey-glazed ham as much as the next red-blooded American man.

On Easter Sunday.

You now find yourself being the one who is shrugging, unsure what there is to say to such a comment. Glancing back to the perhaps-Cambodian woman, you think about the very meaning of Christmas. And the answer seems obvious. "Because Christmas is about tradition."

"Isn't Christmas about the birth of Christ?"

"Well, yes. At least that was how it started. But now it's about so much more."

"It's about giving," Taryl says, as if she is a pupil attempting to answer a question.

"Yes, but that's because giving is part of the tradition. But it all comes back to tradition. And turkey is part of that tradition."

"But what if I don't really like that part of the tradition? Can't I change it?"

You shake your head. "I don't think you can just change tradition on a whim. Otherwise it wouldn't be a tradition."

"It's not on a whim. I've always liked ham more than turkey. Although I do enjoy all the other things. The potatoes. The corn. The dressing—"

"But dressing is traditionally cooked inside a turkey."

"I think that's stuffing, not dressing."

"I think that's the same thing."

Taryl shrugs and raises both palms to the air. "I don't know. Maybe it's just our family. But everyone is different. You have chili pepper jelly on crackers on Christmas Eve, right?"

"With Philadelphia Cream Cheese."

"Yes. But that's your tradition. And I'm sure that Oriental lady there has her own traditions on Christmas. Maybe spring rolls with cranberry sauce? You never know."

Although again wary of the perhaps-Singaporean lady overhearing, you also think that Taryl might just be onto something. If spring rolls are delicious when dipped into plum sauce (and you're still not sure how this could be primarily composed of pumpkin), then why not cranberry sauce? Now you're even more excited about bringing home that Oriental appetizer party pack. This could be a new Christmas Eve appie party tradition in the making, right up there with Ann's famous holiday punch.

And then it strikes you: maybe Taryl isn't so crazy? Maybe you are the one too set in your ways? When you were a young man, you weren't so rigid in your thinking. The first time you heard Chumbawamba's *Tubthumping*, you shouldn't have given the song the time of day. It sounded nothing like anything Hootie and the Blowfish had ever released. But you let yourself go. The crowd around you got up onto their feet and started dancing. Never before had you moved to music like this, and yet you joined them. You let go of your reservations. And it was true. When you got knocked down, you got up again.

What was the last new song you heard that really spoke to you in any way? You can't even think of one. All that confectionary pop that Emma listens to all sounds the same. Often you can't even tell if it's a man or a woman singing. And you've expressed these thoughts to others on many occasions: there just isn't any good new music anymore. But what if you'd never before heard Chumbawamba? And what if the raucous beat of *Tubthumping* came on the speakers at the grocery store—right then? Would you even notice? Would the melody strike a chord with you? Or would it just be another part of the background? Another sign of the decline of modern music, modern society?

You know the answer.

You wouldn't give it the time of day.

It's hard not to sigh. If you've been wrong about the meaning of tradition, then you've been wrong about the meaning of Christmas. Perhaps you don't know the meaning of Christmas? Perhaps—if people can have ham and others can dip their spring rolls in cranberry sauce—then there is no meaning to Christmas?

This can't be. You've seen far too many holiday television specials for it to mean nothing. Even Quantum Leap did its take on *A Christmas Carol*. No, if you struggle to find a meaning to Christmas, it is because you need to keep searching, not because the meaning is non-existent. Your job is to find it.

"So," Taryl asks, "will that be cash or credit?"

"Credit, of course." You say with a grin, looking forward to the extra travel points you'll get on your MasterCard Titanium. One point per dollar means you're now almost sixty points closer to the next reward. Each time it may not be much, but it adds up. Not that you need to pay for flights, of course, but you can apply the points towards hotels, making your holidays fantastic bargains that most of your friends can only dream of. Just last year you visited the Calgary Stampede, and when taking into account the devalued Canadian currency, it was perhaps the least-expensive family vacation you'd ever had. Probably not the finest holiday, but certainly the cheapest. After withdrawing your MasterCard Titanium from your wallet, you swipe it through the machine. It beeps. It's hard to tell from just a single note, but something about the frequency leads you to believe that there is a problem.

"Is something wrong?" You ask.

"Oh, did it beep?"

"Yeah, it beeped."

"Kinda of a groaning sort of beep?"

"It had a little bit of chirp to it."

"Mind trying again?"

"It's not going to charge me twice?"

Taryl chuckles, almost dismissive. "No, they can't do that."

Although you don't care for her cavalier attitude, or her implicit faith in credit card technology, you again swipe through your MasterCard Titanium, certain that you'll double-check the receipt when all of this is done.

It beeps in a way that, you have to admit, has a slight groaning quality to it.

"Yup," Taryl says. "That means you can't swipe. But you can tap your card."

"I can tap it?"

"Yeah, just tap it against the screen. It's new."

You're hesitant. "I know it's popular in Europe, but I've never used it here. It sounds woefully lacking in security."

"Yeah, but it's not like we really ever used to check a person's signature."

"I'm pretty sure some people would."

Taryl shakes her head. "Nah. We'd just pretend."

"Really?"

"Yeah. So, don't worry. Just tap it and go. It's really fast. Saves lots of time."

You do like the idea of time being saved from your busy life. Even just a few seconds here and there—like travel points on your MasterCard Titanium—it all adds up. Okay. You're going to do it. You hold out your credit card, delicately bring it towards the terminal with the steady hand of a pilot landing a 747... and it beeps.

"That worked," Taryl says with a wink.

"That was pretty slick. And so very fast."

"Personally, I think it's great. It's faster than cash."

You nod, thinking of the time you came here without your MasterCard Titanium and were forced to pay cash. There was absolutely nothing expedient about that entire process—although, to be honest, you wonder if this is taking even longer. You look at the time on your phone. It's 5:31. You were supposed to be home a minute ago. Even the most time-efficient payment systems won't be enough to afford you negative time.

"Well," Taryl grabs the receipt as it ejects from the register and then holds it towards you. "Do you want the receipt or can I put it in the bag?"

You're about to dismiss the offer until remembering that you double-swiped your MasterCard Titanium. "I'll take it, actually." You unfurl the paper, eyes drawn to the bottom.

Sub-Total:	54.10
Tax:	4.60
Total:	58.70
Credit Tend:	58.70
Change Due:	0.00

While annoyed by the additional $4.60 in tax that is being tacked on to your bill for no apparent benefit to your life, you are pleased that, by all indications, your MasterCard Titanium has been charged only once. However, you then feel that it would be prudent to survey the entire receipt. Considering how many times Taryl became distracted, the chances of her running through something in error seems quite probable.

Loaf of Flax Plus Bread	6.39
Plastic Bag	0.10
Hot Pepper Jelly	7.49
Philadelphia Cream Cheese Spread 8 oz	2.99
Triscuit Cracker Original Family Sized	3.99
Quaker Rolled Oats 32 oz	6.99
Sun-Maid Raisins Natural California 32 oz	6.19
Sun-Maid Raisins Natural California 32 oz	6.19
Kellogg's Cornflakes 26.8 oz	2.89

General Grocery	2.99
Potatoes Russet Bulk 2.58 lbs	3.40
7-Up Cranberry Soda 12-12 oz	4.49
Sub-Total:	54.10
Tax:	4.60
Total:	58.70
Credit Tend:	58.70
Change Due:	0.00

Wait! A ten cent charge for a plastic bag? Taryl didn't make any mention of this. "Excuse me, but I see here that there is a charge for the plastic bag?"

"Yeah. I think it's, like, an environmental thing." She sighs, shaking her head. "Taxes." And she says nothing more, as if that single word was a thorough explanation.

"Is it really a tax or is it just a charge?"

"I don't know."

"If it was a tax then the same amount would be levied at all stores. But I don't think that's the case." Right as you say this, you fear that you've been paying this additional ten-cent charge for months, maybe years? You think of all the times cashiers would ask if you wanted a bag and you almost always replied with an affirmative. Was there a ten-cent charge being applied to every single one of those transactions? If this is the case, then when was this environmental law passed? Was it one of those endless propositions in the last election? Did you actually vote in favor of this intrusive, overbearing tax without realizing it? And if not—if it is just some arbitrary charge that this particular store has deemed to be a worthy expense for the customer—then how exactly did they come to this ten-cent price point? Surely the cost of the plastic must be mere pennies. And significantly less than ten pennies. Which means that this supermarket is profiting from something under the guise of being environmentally conscious. No matter the cause of this exorbitant fee, you feel incensed. Or, at least mild-to-moderately annoyed.

Taryl says, "I didn't charge you for the second, if that makes you feel any better."

This does not make you feel any better. If you recall correctly, Taryl didn't even give you a choice. She just double-bagged your items. "I just never noticed this before."

"I'm pretty sure we've been charging it for over a year now."

"Really?"

"Yeah."

"That long?"

"Uh huh."

"Huh."

"Yeah."

"Hmm," you add with a gentle nod, although you still don't believe her.

"If you really want," Taryl says, reaching towards the screen. "I can reimburse your credit card for the amount."

"No," you quickly reply, not wanting to sound so petty or cheap. "That's okay." Now that this store has successfully swindled another ten cents from your bank account, you decide to check over the receipt again, this time with a careful eye for detail, starting at the very top:

Loaf of Flax Plus Bread	6.39
Plastic Bag	0.10
Hot Pepper Jelly	7.49

Seven and a half dollars for a jar of jelly? Was it really that much? You don't recall looking at the price when you grabbed it from the shelf, but that seems like highway robbery.

"Everything all right?" Taryl asks.

"Oh yeah. Just checking."

"Take your time," she says while retrieving her phone.

Oh, you're going to take your time, all right. Now, where were you? Yes, overpriced jelly.

Hot Pepper Jelly	7.49
Philadelphia Cream Cheese Spread 8 oz	2.99
Triscuit Crackers Original Family Sized	3.99

Less than four dollars for a family-sized box of delicious Triscuits? You smile, pleased with the bargain, although unsure if this compensates for the chili pepper jelly.

Quaker Rolled Oats 32 oz	6.99
Sun-Maid Raisins Natural California 32 oz	6.19
Sun-Maid Raisins Natural California 32 oz	6.19

Did you really need more than twelve dollars' worth of Sun-Maid Raisins?

Yes.

Kellogg's Cornflakes 26.8 oz	2.89

Now *that* is a fantastic bargain. Too bad Taryl didn't ring in that more than once. You would happily accept several more of those.

General Grocery	2.99

You look back to Taryl. "Excuse me."

"One sec," she says while furiously typing.

You nod, as if to say, "*Of course*," and look back towards the perhaps-Tibetan woman, who continues to hold her quart of buttermilk, staring ahead without any sign of being annoyed by the time you are taking at the checkout. You feel like you should at least offer her some form of apology, even if she doesn't seem perturbed (and even if you are not actually sorry, since it is because of Taryl, not you, that this entire escapade is taking so long). "Sorry," you say to the customer, but she doesn't react. You're not sure if she didn't hear you or simply doesn't understand what you're saying. Trying again, this time you lean forward. "Sorry about this taking so long."

She flinches and then nods with quick, intense pivots, appearing frightened of you, her reaction one of nervous appeasement. What does she think is happening here? Has she mistaken you for a member of some sort of ruling elite, a man of such lofty societal stature that one never expresses any degree of dissatisfaction or frustration? If you were dressed in your pilot's uniform, then this would seem to be a much more probable situation. But you're wearing nothing exceptional: a navy-blue cardigan with a powder-blue Oxford shirt and beige khakis. Of course, your winter jacket covers most of your outfit. All she can see are your slate-blue boat shoes and khakis up to the thigh. Maybe you should unzip your coat? Now that you think about it, you are quite warm and it might feel good to air things out a bit. You slide down the zipper, almost down to the bottom, but are unsure if you should unhitch it entirely.

After all, you're going to be heading back to your Volvo sedan any minute now. You wave the collar and smile back towards the perhaps-Mongolian woman.

You then notice a faint smell of body odor. Crap. Is that you? You know you showered this morning—you lathered with body wash, you ran shampoo and conditioner through your hair, you brushed your teeth (didn't floss)—but did you put on deodorant? You pretend to search within a pocket on the inside of your jacket, leaning and inhaling deeply. The twangy punch of body odor is unmistakable. It has been resolved: you neglected to apply underarm deodorant this morning. You zip your jacket back up, right to the collar, aware that such an action will only intensify your perspiration, but hopefully also contain that pungent funk. What physical activity did you engage in today to warrant such a stench? You didn't work-out. You didn't perform any heavy labor. The most exhausting thing you've done was carry these groceries to the till. Has your general level of health deteriorated so much that the simple act of picking up groceries now causes you to sweat as if you're being forced to run ten miles? Now *that* is a disaster.

"What's up?" Taryl asks while placing her phone onto the counter beside the register.

You're definitely not about to relay your concerns regarding your general health and odor, but you can't remember just what you wanted to ask her in the first place. You look down to the receipt gripped between the thumb and forefinger of your right hand, knowing that it had something to do with the items purchased. "I actually forgot what I was going to ask."

"That happens to me all the time. I guess it wasn't all that important, right?" Taryl adds with a lighthearted chuckle.

"That's what I always say to my daughter. It doesn't make her feel better. In fact, it annoys her more."

"How old is she again?"

"She's nine, but going on—"

"Sixteen?"

"Yeah. Did I say that already?"

"I think you did."

Fair enough. With a line that witty and appropriate, how can you *not* use it more than once?

Taryl then says, "It's funny," with an assuring nod.

You nod in genuine agreement, but then realize that you still don't know what you wanted to ask her. You could let it go, take your groceries and move on, but you're also aware that if you had something to ask, then there was a good reason for it. Contrary to what Taryl said to you (and what you say to your daughter), if you are going to ask someone a question, then you have a good reason for doing so. You return to the receipt.

Loaf of Flax Plus Bread	6.39
Plastic Bag	0.10
Hot Pepper Jelly	7.49
Philadelphia Cream Cheese Spread 8 oz	2.99
Triscuit Cracker Original Family Sized	3.99
Quaker Rolled Oats 32 oz	6.99
Sun-Maid Raisins Natural California 32 oz	6.19
Sun-Maid Raisins Natural California 32 oz	6.19
Kellogg's Cornflakes 26.8 oz	2.89
General Grocery	2.99
Potatoes Russet Bulk 2.58 lbs	3.40
7-Up Cranberry Soda 12-12 oz	4.49

Oh yes! "That was it," you say. "I was going to ask you what this 'General Grocery' charge was." You hold the paper out towards Taryl, your thumbnail underlining the item.

Her expression makes it clear that she, too, cannot remember. She purses her lips and looks down into the bag of your items. "Was it the potatoes?"

"No, they are listed right here, second from the bottom."

"Huh."

"Yeah. I thought about that myself, for a moment."

"It wasn't the 7-Up, was it?"

You shake your head with an apologetic frown. "Nope. That's the last thing on the receipt."

"I remember putting it in for something, right?"

"I remember that, too."

Taryl continues to stare into the bag, shaking her head ever so slowly. You wonder if she might decide to offer you a full refund for this mysterious item—although considering that you've already paid for all the groceries, this would probably be a little too time consuming to be of any benefit.

"I guess I can offer you a refund on it," she then says.

As with any other red-blooded American man, the last thing you'd ever want to be considered is cheap, but you are also a man of principle, a man of honor, traits fostered and honed from your time in the military. If this employee cannot recall just what she charged you for, then it should be her responsibility to rectify the situation. You pretend to dismiss her offer with a casual bat of one hand, assuming she will make the same offer again. "I don't think that should be necessary. After all, I've already paid for the goods. And I thought you can't cancel items?"

"No, I can do this. I just need to swipe your credit card again. Now that the transaction is complete, I'm pretty sure I can still redeem your card the $2.99."

"Plus 8.5 percent sales tax."

"Yeah," she says, seemingly both surprised and uncertain about how to calculate such a thing.

"I mean, it's not that I care. But if you're going to redeem, you might as well include the tax. I don't want the government taking any more of my money than they already do, right?"

"I hear you on that one," she says, shaking her head again. "I swear, all we do is pay taxes, and I don't know where any of it goes."

"It's just one boondoggle to the next with these politicians."

"Or one war to the next, right?" she says with a snarky grin.

You don't find this comment funny or appropriate. "I was in the Air Force for many years."

"Oh. Yeah. Well, that's different, right?"

"Terrorism doesn't stop itself, does it?"

"No. Sorry."

"Don't mention it." Now that she has sullied the good name of your former career, you are definitely going to get your hard-earned money back. "So, I think I might take you up on the offer to redeem."

"Okay. So, that would be 2.99 plus... how much tax?"

"Eight and a half percent."

"Oh yeah. So," she pulls out an old calculator from beside the till, one with large buttons appropriate for a young child and a thin solar-panel strip above the display. "How would I calculate that?"

"It's probably easiest just to type 2.99 and then multiply by 1.085."

"Oh yeah," she says again. "It's been awhile since I took a math class."

You are tempted to ask if she can still read, considering that it's likely been awhile since she's taken an English class, but choose to keep this thought to yourself. She jabs the buttons of the calculators with enough force to rattle the plastic, then looks at the screen, pauses, and then says: "Okay. So, I guess that comes to five dollars and fifty-three cents? That doesn't sound right."

"That's definitely not right."

"Oh!" She snaps her fingers once. "I forgot to hit the percent button." She presses the button, reads the screen, and her joyous expression sinks. "That doesn't make sense." She holds up the calculator. In block numbers, the display reads: 0.055315

You say, "That's like, five and a half cents."

"Oh yeah. Okay, let me try that again." She batters the all-clear button several times and then types, saying it aloud: "Two-point-nine-nine times one-point-eight-five."

"Ah," you interject. "That's the problem."

"I know. I still have to hit the percent button."

"That's not the problem."

She nods and smiles, hits the percent button, and then frowns. "I have the same thing as before."

"It's because you missed a zero."

"Did I?"

"You should be multiplying by one-point-*zero*-eight-five."

"What did I say?"

"One-point-eight-five."

She seems wary of your advice, but nonetheless clears the calculator screen with another series of aggressive pecks at the All-Clear, and then vocalizes each number as she presses the appropriate button: "So, two-point-nine-nine times one-point," she then looks back at you. "What is that again?

You hold out your hand, "Why don't I just type it in?"

Taryl grabs the calculator, ready to pass it over, but then hesitates. "I don't think I should."

"Why's that?"

"I doubt company policy would allow a customer to calculate his own bill."

"But I'm telling you what to type, right?"

"Yeah," she nods but soon shakes her head. "I know, but I still don't feel right about it." Her eyebrows then rise, "Why don't I just call over Misty? She can tell me."

"No, no, no. This has all taken long enough. I don't want to cause any troubles."

"Okay." She puts the calculator back down in front of her. "So, two-point-nine-nine times one-point," she then looks to you.

"Zero-eight-five."

She repeats, "Zero-eight-five, and then, equals." She looks at the screen, winces for a moment and then nods. "Okay. So, that will be four dollars and twenty-one cents."

"That can't be right."

"Maybe the math is wrong?"

"No, it's grade school math. It's not wrong."

"What grade, you think?"

Good question. You have a distinct memory of sitting at your scuffed wooden desk with a Casio calculator in front of you. It was a big deal, being *allowed* to use a calculator in class. Until then, such technology was the domain of the naughty, those kids who snuck them on their laps and used them for basic arithmetic while the rest of you chugged away at long multiplication like a bunch of suckers. But one day, they became permitted. You could type 58008 as many times as you'd wish and no one could tell you to put the device away. What was the name of the teacher? You remember his face: rectangular with a strong chin, light stubble, and stern, solid eyebrows. A big man who walked as if on patrol, arms always folded and accenting his gut. Mr. Sturlubok was his name. "I think I learned it back in the sixth grade."

"Really? I thought it would be more like the eighth or ninth."

"I can remember the teacher. I know he taught me in the sixth grade."

"You remember the teacher?" She says, surprised.

"Yeah."

"You must have a good memory."

You assume that this is a backhanded compliment, recognizing that you would have been in the sixth grade many, many years ago. You're not sure what to say.

"Oh, shoot." Taryl says, "I didn't mean it like that."

"Like what?"

"Like, that you're so old that I wouldn't expect you to remember your sixth grade teacher's name."

You force out a chuckle. "Oh, no. I didn't take it like that." Now you want to know just how she intended you to take her comment and await her explanation.

She gives no explanation. "So, what was his name?"

"The teacher?"

"Yeah."

"Sturlubok."

Taryl shakes her head. "I don't think I know him."

"I didn't think you would."

"Yeah, but I had to ask. You know what they say, right? It's a small world."

You've always actually been very adamant that the world is very, very large. As a pilot with more than twenty-five years of experience, you figure that you are somewhat of an expert on this matter. "Yeah," you say with a limp smile.

"Yeah," Taryl nods back, seeming to forget just what to do next. "Oh yeah, the refund. So, you don't think four dollars and twenty one cents makes sense?"

"It's definitely too much."

"Let me hit the percent button."

"It's not that."

Regardless of your comment, Taryl hits the percent button. "I don't think that's right."

"You don't need to hit the percent button."

"What does the percent button do, then?"

"I don't actually know."

"Huh. So, what do you think the problem is?"

"Did you hit the clear button?"

Taryl snaps her fingers. "Maybe that was it. Let me try again." She hits that AC button at least ten times. "Two-point-nine-nine times one-point," she then looks at you.

"Zero-eight-five."

"So, one-point-*zero*-eight-five and equals." She pressed the final button, leans back, and then looks back to you, uncertain. "I'm not sure."

"What does it say?"

"Three dollars and twenty-four cents."

"That sounds right."

"Does it?"

"Yeah."

"Okay. So, three dollars and twenty-four cents as a refund to your credit card." Taryl repeats, nods to show her acceptance of this amount and taps a few points on the screen. She then stops. "Wait a minute."

"Is there a problem?"

"I just remembered what that 'General Grocery' was for."

"What was it?"

"The Oriental appetizer party pack. Remember, we didn't know the UPC, so I just put it in for $2.99. Heck of a bargain, really."

Taryl is correct, and you are feeling doubly shameful about this. First, because you now appear cheap for your insistence on getting the measly 25-cent sales tax refunded. And second, because a simple grocery store cashier apparently possesses a better memory than you (although not when it comes to calculating percentages). "Yes, that was it."

"And I presume you're still going to pick it up before you leave, you know, along with the two bags of raisins and box of corn flakes?"

If you now insist that you don't need the Oriental appetizer party pack, then all this time spent on sales tax calculations would not be rendered moot. You are tempted. It also might make you seem *less* cheap—after all, didn't Taryl pressure you into buying the Oriental appetizer party pack? To be honest, you really can't remember. It feels like you've spent all of Christmas Eve inside this darn grocery store.

But, no. You want those spring rolls and things in crispy little cups. They are too delicious to leave behind.

"Yeah, I'll still be picking them up."

"All right then." Taryl smiles. "I guess that's it." She passes over the plastic bag and slides the cardboard box of limited edition Cranberry 7-Up.

"I guess so."

"Have a merry Christmas."

Reaching out to clasp the strained loops of the plastic bag, you feel a tingling sensation in your upper left thigh. As usual, your first reaction is to fear that you are having a stroke. And as usual, your subsequent reaction is to realize that you have become far too anxious about health complications in these recent years. Your phone is vibrating. There is hardly a point in looking at who is calling. You know.

You say: "Hey, Honey."

"*Are you okay?*" Ann asks, her tone sounding annoyed, not concerned.

"Yeah, just finishing up here at the store." As you say this, you begin to inspect the contents of the plastic bag—or more accurately, the way in which these contents have been placed. You see no sign of the once-luscious flax seed bread, which means that it has been entirely smothered by the other items.

"*What's taking you so long?*"

Just as you feared—and reminded Taryl about—the bread is crushed beneath the overbearing mass of the oats and potatoes. What was Taryl thinking, putting the bread in first? Although you assume that there is more to being a successful grocery store cashier than simply knowing to place the heaviest items at the bottom of the bag, this really must be one of their prime directives. You sigh, wondering if Taryl should be informed about this. And you also remember something about the phrase, "*prime directives.*" Where had you heard that from? Although sounding vaguely military in origin, you are aware that it is not actually a term that was ever used in your many years of service to your country.

"*Hey,*" Ann says over the phone, "*What's taking you so long?*"

Crap. Now Ann is going to think that you've been thinking of an excuse. "Sorry, it's been really busy. You know, Christmas Eve shoppers, and all."

"*Really?*" She doesn't believe you.

"Yeah, sorry. I was just distracted there for a moment." You turn to face away from Taryl and whisper into the phone: "The cashier did a terrible job of packing the groceries."

"*So, you're done now?*"

"Yeah. Well, pretty much. I still have to pick up a couple of things."

"*So, you're not finished?*"

"I've already paid for it."

"*How?*"

"Oh, it's a long and crazy story. I'll tell you all about it when I get home."

"*You said you would be home, like, twenty minutes ago.*"

You look at the time on your phone. "I said I'd be home more like ten minutes ago."

"*And by the time you are finished there, it will be more like twenty minutes.*"

More like twenty-five, you think, but refrain from admitting this. You pull out the jar of chili pepper jelly, the potatoes, and then the bag of Quaker rolled oats, laying them on the counter as Taryl asks the perhaps-North-Korean lady if she will need a bag.

"*Are you listening?*" Ann says and you were definitely not listening. Your mind is distracted by the buttermilk purchase, the terrible packing of your groceries, and one other thing.

You say into the phone: "Hey, can I ask you a question?"

"*What?*"

"Do you know where the phrase, *'Prime Directive'* comes from?"

Ann sighs. *"I assume it's from Quantum Leap?"*

You reply with patronizing certainty: "No, it's not from Quantum Leap."

"Why are you asking?"

"It's just something that's been on my mind just now."

"It's from Star Trek," Taryl says, surprising you.

"Is it?" You reply, never really a fan of any of the many incarnations of Star Trek and therefore doubtful that this is what you'd been thinking about.

Taryl nods, again completely ignoring the perhaps-Taiwanese lady. "Yeah, the Prime Directive of the Federation is that they should never interfere with alien civilizations. I'm a bit of a Trekkie, what can I say?"

You have to admit that this does sound familiar. "I thought the term is Trekker, not Trekkie?"

"Oh, I think Trekker just sounds stupid. I prefer Trekkie."

Just how *Trekker* can be deemed as being stupid and yet somehow *Trekkie* entirely appropriate, you cannot understand. To be honest, they both sound stupid.

"What are you talking about?" Ann asks.

"Oh, Taryl was just telling me about the term, *prime directive.*"

"Who is Taryl?"

"The cashier."

"You're on a first-name basis with her?"

"I have been here for some time."

You can hear Ann groan. *"Well, I'm glad that you've figured out where 'Prime Imperative' comes from."*

"It's prime directive, not prime imperative."

Ann doesn't reply.

You add, "And, to be honest, I don't think that's it. I feel like it's from something else."

Taryl interjects, "Oh, trust me, it's from Star Trek."

"I believe you." You don't believe her. "It's just that I think it's also from something else."

"What do you think it's from?" Taryl asks.

"I don't know. That's why I've been asking," you say, figuring that such a reply really need not be stated. And you also figure that Taryl should spend her time focusing on her current customer—or at least ask why you've taken out several groceries from your bag.

Ann asks, "*Are you coming home now?*"

"Yes, yes." You rearrange the loaf of bread so that it now stands on one end, and place the chili pepper jelly, oats and potatoes back around it so as to hold it upright. All along, you assume that Taryl might interject some comment about this, but instead she asks the perhaps-Singaporese lady if she will be paying with cash or credit.

"*Did you remember to get the wet-wipes?*"

"Oh." Immediately, you regret beginning with this. You know you need to reply straightaway or else Ann will trust nothing of what you say. "They were actually out."

"*Out of wet-wipes?*"

"Yeah. I guess because it's Christmas Eve?"

"*Why would that have anything to do with it? It's not like wet-wipes are given out as Christmas presents.*"

"No, but maybe people need to stock up?" While saying this, you realize that it would actually be quite helpful if you were to receive a pack of wet-wipes for Christmas. Should someone else want to pay for such a thing, then you would gladly accept them into your home.

"*I don't think people need to stock up on wet-wipes. Did you even check?*"

"Of course I did."

Taryl asks, "Is everything alright?"

You want to tell her that she should have done a better job packing the groceries and you deserve a refund (with sales tax) on the now flattened bread. But you need to get home. "Oh, everything is fine."

"*Don't say everything is fine. Trust me. We need those wet-wipes.*"

"No, I was talking to the cashier."

"*You mean Taryl?*"

You cannot avoid sighing. "Yes, her."

Taryl says, "If you forgot something, you can go pick it up and I'll run it through."

"No, I didn't forget anything."

"*Yes, you did.*"

"No, they were just out of stock."

"Out of stock of what?" Taryl asks.

"Never mind."

Taryl seems annoyed by your dismissive reply. "Sorry," she says in a way that is very clearly not apologetic.

"*Well, sorry.*" Ann says in a way that is very clearly not apologetic.

"No, I wasn't talking to you."

"Oh," says Taryl.

"*Oh,*" says Ann.

Now even you are not sure just whom you were speaking to. And again, your attention returns to Taryl's current customer, the perhaps-Laotian woman, to which Taryl is again asking if she has a customer club card, pronouncing her words with slow and deliberate syllables. The quart of buttermilk rests on the counter. You cannot imagine how this woman would have any interest in purchasing buttermilk for her household. It must be a mistake. What if she returned home, ready to make a family meal, only to ruin it with that rotten, disgusting form of milk? This grocery store is due to close in just over an hour. Nothing would be open tomorrow. This woman's Christmas—and perhaps her very first Christmas in the United States of America—would be ruined, all because no one stepped up to tell her just what she was purchasing.

You joined the military to make the world a better place, one sortie at a time. Now with all of that behind you, perhaps it is time to make the world a better place, one quart of milk at a time? Perhaps this, right here, is your chance to discover the true meaning of Christmas?

"*Well?*" Ann says, clearly referring to some question she'd asked, to which you hadn't paid attention.

"Just wait," You put down the phone and wave towards the perhaps-Burmese/Myanma lady, who is receiving her change from Taryl. "Excuse me?"

Taryl looks towards you, "Is there something else wrong?"

"No, I actually want to talk to your customer." Again you wave and sustain eye contact with the elderly lady. You have depleted your knowledge of east-Asian countries and do not know what else to call her. "Excuse me, but I think you bought the wrong type of milk."

She looks at you, shakes her head, and says, "Sorry," as if you are trying to sell her something.

"No, no. You don't understand." You say, appreciating the irony of her likely not understanding what you just said, and point towards her milk. "That is no good. Yucky."

She nods, then shakes her head and looks back towards Taryl as if for an explanation.

Taryl has returned to her phone, repressing a chuckle while typing a message.

Most people would have given up at this point. Most people would have taken their groceries and headed back to the parking lot. Most people would have rationalized that there was, in fact, a likely scenario where an elderly lady from some distant part of the world would purposely purchase a quart of buttermilk on Christmas Eve.

But most people would have never done half the things you've done in your life. Most people have never even flown a plane, let alone pilot a stealth F-117 Nighthawk into Iraqi airspace. Most people have never been forced to break another man's neck with just one's bare feet. Most people think that wet-wipes are a necessity. Most people think that Sprite and 7-Up are interchangeable. Most people don't even appear to be able to calculate sales tax. No, you are most definitely not most people.

You return the phone to your ear, "Sorry, Ann. I have to do something. I'll be home in fifteen minutes."

"What are you doing?"

"What am I doing?" You say, as if asking yourself. "I'm showing one of our newest citizens just what the Christmas season is all about."

"And what is it all about, exactly?"

You didn't expect Ann to ask this question and shake your head. "It's hard to put into words. See you soon." You hang up the phone, slide it into your pocket, and spring into action—grabbing the quart of buttermilk from the counter and holding it tight against your coat, a football that you are not about to give up. "I'll be right back."

The elderly lady says something in some language that is not English and you assure her with a firm palm to the air that she needs to do nothing more. You will take care of this.

"What are you doing?" Taryl asks, concerned enough for her current customer's well-being to ask a question, but not so much as to put her phone away. "She already paid for that."

"And that's the problem." You then look back towards the elderly woman. "This?" You hold up the buttermilk and pretend to take a sip before wincing and shaking your head. "No good. Bad. Bad milk. Bad." You then point across the grocery store. "I get you good milk." You accent this with a hearty nod and smile. "Good milk. Okay?"

She looks back to Taryl, who just shrugs.

"One minute," you assure the lady and march away from the till with long strides, walking around a deep bin full of bargain DVDs and down towards the far end of the grocery store, where the fluorescent shelves of the refrigerated section beckon you like the radiant nose of Rudolph the Red-Nosed Reindeer (but not red—instead a ghostly white, really). You have a mission to accomplish. You pass the aisle with dried pastas, prepared sauces, and canned beans. You pass the aisle with baking supplies, dried fruits, and sugar. You pass the aisle with soups, canned vegetables and crackers. You pass the aisle with cereals, granola bars and oats.

Wait. You stop, turn, and hurry down this last section, searching for the box of Kellogg's Cornflakes that has already been charged to your MasterCard Titanium. You then remember that you are owed a second bag of Sun-Maid Raisins. *And* the Oriental appetizer party pack. And wasn't there something else? Well, it's a good thing that you kept that receipt!

Loaf of Flax Plus Bread	6.39
Plastic Bag	0.10
Hot Pepper Jelly	7.49
Philadelphia Cream Cheese Spread 8 oz	2.99
Triscuit Cracker Original Family Sized	3.99
Quaker Rolled Oats 32 oz	6.99
Sun-Maid Raisins Natural California 32 oz	6.19
Sun-Maid Raisins Natural California 32 oz	6.19
Kellogg's Cornflakes 26.8 oz	2.89
General Grocery	2.99
Potatoes Russet Bulk 2.58 lbs	3.40
7-Up Cranberry Soda 12-12 oz	4.49

Nope, just the corn flakes, raisins and the Oriental appetizer party pack. You wonder if it might take too long to obtain all of these items before returning to the elderly lady with her (surely) intended quart of regular milk. But the corn flakes are literally right in front of you, so you retrieve the box and check the size. 26.8 ounces, just as stated on the receipt. There is a row of hefty 43-ounce boxes just below, and you cannot deny the temptation to grab one of these instead, but this would go against the very nature of the Christmas season (and you're unselfish act of goodwill). Next, the raisins. Have you passed them already? You know that the Oriental appetizer party pack is in the frozen section (conveniently across from the dairy products), but where were the dried fruits? You emerge from the end of this row of shelves, seeing that the elderly woman is staring at you from the other end of the store. Figuring that she deserves some sort of signal to indicate that progress is being made, you go with a proud and confident thumbs up. You walk towards her, glancing to your right each time to read the displayed food categories for each section. There it is: *baking supplies, dried fruits, and sugars.* In less time than it would take to crack open a can of limited edition Cranberry 7-Up and savor that first sip (which, with any luck, you'll be able to do in under thirty minutes), you locate the 32-ounce bag of Sun-Maid Raisins. Two down, two to go. You're making good time—and as a pilot you appreciate the importance of maintaining a brisk pace in all of life's activities. Returning to the end of the aisle, you resume your trek towards the far side of the store. You think you hear someone calling out from behind, but you don't look back and so figure that you can't be blamed for failing to stop. The temperature of the air drops as you approach your final destination. Pulling open the glass door and unleashing a whirring breeze of cool air, you instinctively grab a quart of 2% and return the elderly lady's erroneously purchased buttermilk. Why on Earth would these two things be shelved so close to one another? Surely this woman is not the first to purchase buttermilk by accident?

But then you wonder if she might be more of a whole milk woman? Or 1%? Or skim? Somehow the idea of that elderly lady wishing to purchase skim milk seems the most preposterous. Did skim milk exist when she was a child? Does skim milk even exist in Asian countries? Come to think of it, aren't most Asians lactose intolerant? You also have the option of taking one of those freakish lactose-free milk products that are now available, but the idea of lactose-free milk just sounds... inappropriate. Like protein-free beef.

Or an electric car. No, you'll go with your instincts. 2% it is. And besides, the lactose-free versions cost almost twice as much and you don't really want to have to go through the whole rigmarole of reimbursing Taryl for anything else. This has taken quite long enough, thank you very much.

A few steps across the aisle brings you to the freezers and the Oriental appetizer party pack. Four spring rolls, four wonton cups, four pork pot-stickers and four vegetable dumplings, all for $7.99. That $2.99 *General Grocery* charge feels more opportune than ever, and you smile, knowing that good things really do happen to good people. Turning over the box to inspect the ingredients, you have to squint to read the miniscule font for details on what exactly constitutes plum sauce. And there, much to your amazement, is the fact of the matter: pureed pumpkin is ahead of plums on the list. Well done, Taryl. Not that you'll mention this to her—that would merely relay your lack of trust in her comment from earlier. Plus, sugar is, indeed, the first ingredient, meaning you were also correct.

Your hands are fully occupied clasping the box of corn flakes, the bag of raisins and the quart of 2% milk, so you tuck the frigid package of appetizers under one arm (aware that you are lacking in antiperspirant but confident that the odor is not so pungent as to traverse your coat and the cardboard packaging) and return to the check-out with a triumphant gait. Taryl is now approaching, waving at you as if you might not notice her presence. "What are you doing?" She asks from a distance. "I was about to call security."

"I didn't know there were security guards here."

"There aren't. We have to call them in from another store."

"That sounds rather useless."

"Well, that's why I didn't call."

"No need for any of that." You hold up the quart of 2% milk. "I was just getting this." The elderly lady from whom you'd taken the buttermilk still waits by the till, looking at you with an expression of terrified confusion. "Here," you hand the milk towards her, but she stares back in silence, shaking her head back and forth. Fair enough. She is confused. She needs you to explain the situation. "This is the right milk. Good milk. Here, take it. Please. Take milk. Good milk. Other milk, bad milk. Bad." You force the plastic jug into her hand and, perhaps reluctantly, she takes it from you. "There you go."

The elderly lady looks towards Taryl, who only shrugs, and then to an old man who is searching through the bin of discount DVDs and seems unaware of what is happening mere feet away.

"You can go home now," you say with a smile. "It is yours."

She nods but doesn't actually move.

Reaching out to pat her shoulder, she flinches back. "Merry Christmas," you say, and then point towards the exits. "You can go now."

She turns and walks away, first slowly, then with a nervous haste. You turn back to Taryl, who has returned to her spot behind the register and is back on her phone, pleased that there is no one else in line. You say, "Well, Taryl, I think that's what Christmas is all about."

"Uh huh," she says, texting.

"Helping out those less fortunate."

Taryl nods.

"By the way, could I get another plastic bag for these last few groceries I just grabbed?"

"Sure," without looking, she grabs a bag from the dispenser and passes it to you. "I won't charge you for it, either."

"Well, thanks."

"'Tis the season."

"*You don't say,*" exudes the old man by the discount DVDs, his voice attracting your attention. He sports wild gray hair and a frizzy white beard that reaches the collar of his sweater. He then laughs—a deep chuckle right from his lungs—and as he stands straight, he displays his rotund belly as if proud of its burgeoning mass. He's dressed in a red sweater with, what looks like a thick, black belt.

He turns and you realize that the red sweater is a stained and faded hoodie with holes in each elbow. What you thought was a belt is actually a garbage bag tied around his waist to hold up his jeans, which are far too large for his lanky legs. You recognize him as a homeless man who frequents this store (although clearly he has put on some weight over these last few years; perhaps the high sugar and fat content in his beloved Sesame Snaps has caught up with him?). He holds up a DVD to Taryl and exclaims, "Only 99 cents! What a bargain."

Taryl replies without looking away from her phone: "Are you actually going to buy that, Randy?"

"I might."

"Do you even have a DVD player?"

"I could get one. They're real cheap these days."

"Okay then, let's ring it through."

Randy seems tempted, but then puts it back down. "Nah, just the Sesame Snap for me." He places a single pack on the conveyor and pulls out a handful of pennies and nickels from his pockets. "But, I tell you, 99 cents for *Robocop* is a deal that can't be beat."

You should be finished here. The elderly woman's buttermilk has been swapped with a more sensible 2%. All your groceries have been acquired (aside from those wet-wipes), purchased (aside from the full-cost of the Oriental appetizer party pack) and bagged (aside from the limited edition Cranberry 7-Up). And yet, it seems that the universe wanted you to linger for a good reason. You turn towards Randy and ask, "Excuse me, but did you say, *Robocop*?"

"Yeah," excitedly, Randy reaches back and holds up the DVD, the original 1987 version with the poker-faced chrome cyborg emerging from his squad car and staring at the camera while the night lights of Old Detroit shimmer in the distance. Or is that Delta City? You're really not sure. But, man, did you love that movie when you were a teenager. Randy then hands it towards you. "You should buy it."

Although 99 cents is a fantastic bargain (and who doesn't love a bargain?), you do not see why you would pay for any DVD these days, since just about anything can be streamed on Netflix. "No thanks."

"You sure? It's a great film."

"Oh, I know."

"Then you should buy it. Really, what else can you get for just 99 cents?"

The hobo makes a lot of sense, and you have to admit that you are tempted. But your interest was not piqued by the idea of purchasing a DVD, but by the movie itself. "No, you see I was asking Taryl here where the term, *'Prime Directives'* comes from."

"It comes from Star Trek," she says, still on her phone.

"I'm sure you're right," you say, although you are not actually sure of anything that Taryl says (except the bit about pumpkins in plum sauce; you'll give her that one). "But I wasn't thinking about Star Trek. I was thinking about—"

Randy interjects, "Robocop."

"Exactly."

Randy says, "Yeah, it's his fourth directive that gets him into so much trouble. That's the one where he can't arrest any OCP executives. Shuts him down."

You are both impressed and disheartened that this Randy fellow knows so much about Robocop. Surely someone with that good of a memory could do more with his life than this? "That is exactly it. Thank you."

"For what?" he asks.

"For reminding me where that phrase came from. It would have bothered me for days."

Taryl says into her phone, "You could have just Googled it."

"Yes, but this is better. Anyhow, I should be going." You lift your bag of groceries up in an attempt to wave. "Have a merry Christmas."

"You, too." Taryl says without emotion.

"I'm Jewish." Randy says.

"Huh," you say, initially surprised that a homeless man proclaims to practice Judaism. You then realize that your sense of shock might be a sign of religious typecasting, and hope that you are not inadvertently being discriminatory. "Well, then, Happy Holidays."

"You, too." Taryl says without emotion.

"Oh, I don't mind if you say, merry Christmas," Randy says with a shrug. "Doesn't bother me at all. Just thought I'd let it be known that I don't really celebrate the holiday."

"Well, then, Merry Christmas."

"You, too." Taryl says without emotion.

"Merry Christmas," Randy says while unwrapping his package of Sesame Snaps. You then notice that he slips the DVD of Robocop into the front pocket of his hoodie while Taryl continues to focus on her phone. He gives you a wink and you let him have it, choosing to return to your Volvo sedan without saying a word to anyone about this (and it's not like there is any security around to do anything about it, either). 'Tis the season, after all.

The End

■   ■   ■

If you can trust an airplane's auto-pilot with the lives of hundreds of passengers, then perhaps you should trust a self-checkout machine with efficiently and accurately charging you for your eight items? You take the few steps over to claim your spot in the line, watching Turkey Man as he rolls up to till number nine. He looks at you with a blank expression, maintaining eye contact for just a fleeting moment before moving on. And you know what this means. The race is on.

There are six people ahead of you in line, and three in front of Turkey Man. However, you notice one of the customers at a self-checkout machine is already finished his duties: a message on the screen reminds people to take their bags, the receipt dangles from the machine, and the light above him flashes to declare a free till. But this man—you are tempted to describe him as white, middle-aged and a little overweight, although you also fear that this is exactly how others would characterize you—is instead fixated on putting his credit card back in a very specific spot in his wallet. Does he not realize that there are people waiting? That it is Christmas Eve? That every minute of one's life is precious and should not be wasted?

Oh. Perhaps he did realize this, as he puts away his wallet, grabs his groceries, and leaves. The next customer then takes his spot (another man; no further descriptions needed) and has his customer club card ready, wastes no time in declaring that he will not be requiring any bags and then scans his first item—a bag of Quaker rolled oats. You look down to your own basket and see the identical bag. Good man, you think. And then the line lurches forward as another till opens up. Seconds later, there is another. In less time than it takes to savor a couple of gulps of 7-Up, you are at the front. It's amazing! You glance over to Turkey Man and he can't bring himself to look your way. Your lips form a subtle smile, pleased not only with your decision to enter this line, but also with the fact that you are the type of person who makes the correct decisions in life, who trusts his gut, who has the instincts of a winner. The rustling of plastic bags then draws your attention towards a woman with black hair in tight curls. When she turns, having collected her two bags of groceries from her self-checkout till, you are surprised to see that she is at least forty years of age, considerably older and less attractive than you thought when observing her from behind. She makes eye contact with you for the briefest of moments before continuing towards the exit. While perhaps slightly disappointed that her gaze didn't connect with you for a longer period of time (surely she didn't expect you to be younger and more attractive, too, did she?), you are pleased that it is now your turn to scan your goods. With long strides, you carry your groceries to the newly vacated till and start by placing down your 12-pack of limited edition Cranberry 7-Up with a conspicuous thump in an attempt to attract the attention of Turkey Man. It works. He glances towards you and you tap the screen to get started. Mission Accomplished.

After scanning your customer club card to ensure you get the lowest price on all your items, you start with the 7-Up, holding it in the air, watching the red lasers drape parallel lines along the surface until hearing the satisfying beep of acknowledgement. You swipe through the loaf of bread and, again, the machine swiftly recognizes the barcode. You are impressed with how much this technology has improved over these last years, as every single item—the chili pepper jelly, the Triscuits, the rolled oats, the cream cheese, the raisins—is picked up by the scanner with ease. Even the bulk potatoes don't pose any complications. Not knowing the code, you are given a surprisingly vast number of choices for the type and select russet (mostly based on the fact that it is the cheapest option). *2.58 pounds of Russet Potatoes*, the screen reads. That is it, and you reach over to press the virtual *finished* button, but then pause to inspect the transparent bag of potatoes, taking note of its mass. You then sigh.

Chances are, you will gain *more* than 2.58 pounds by the conclusion of this holiday season. 2.58 pounds of fat, not russet potatoes. You try to imagine how a 2.58 pound bag of flab would appear, and then visualize that around your waist.

You really should have purchased the Diet 7-Up, regardless of Ann's apprehension about aspartame. But there is no going back now. You admit to the machine that you used two plastic bags (after which you are told that you are going to be charged a total of 20 cents for that!) and decide to pay with credit. While annoyed that customers must now shell out an extra 10 cents for what are nearly-weightless sheets of cheap plastic, your transaction is swiftly approved and the message "*Happy Holidays*" appears on the screen. It's a nice touch that you didn't expect, raising your spirits and (almost) cancelling out any misgivings about being charged for the plastic bags. Looking back towards the staffed check-outs, where Turkey Man still waits, you take your two bags and depart for the parking lot. Happy Holidays, indeed.

* * *

It's a quarter to six when you arrive home and two sports cars are parked on the street in front of your house. One you recognize immediately—Carlos' no-longer-gleaming chrome Jaguar XKR. Guests were told to arrive any time after 5:30, and knowing how punctual he is, you are not at all surprised to see that Carlos has already arrived. And although he is still someone you consider to be one of your closest friends, you cannot deny that you are somewhat disappointed to know that he chose to attend the party. Ever since his accident, he has not been the same man. Sometimes it is simpler to not see him in person, for then you do not have to think about how much things have changed. The other car—a very-much-so-gleaming blue Audi R8—is more mysterious. It is a beautiful, powerful beast of a car and you avoid making it obvious that you are staring at it as you roll up the driveway.

Emerging from the garage and into the front foyer of your house, you are immediately struck by Kimberley Locke's jangly rendition of *Up on the Housetop* playing over the living room speakers. Once again, satellite radio's pre-selected assortment of holiday favorites never fails to find the perfect song. You smell the sweet aroma of frying onions and feel certain as to what this means: Ann is putting the finishing touches on her ranch and caramelized-onion cheeseball. You then hear the patter of excited steps as Liam scampers towards you, dressed in only a shirt (that reads *"Grandpa's Favorite Xmas Present"*; thank you, Carter's) and a diaper that swings from between his knees like a sack full of coins. "Hi, Daddy," he exclaims before adding, "I had a poop."

Before you can think of a reply (which is difficult), Ann calls out from the kitchen: "You need to change Liam's diaper. I'm busy right now putting the finishing touches on the ranch and caramelized-onion cheeseball."

You knew it! Your olfactory sense has once again proved you correct.

"Daddy?" Liam says with an urgency which implies that you have yet to notice his presence.

"Yes, Liam?"

"I had a poop."

You sigh. "Yes, Liam."

He then turns and hurries up the steps, presumably towards the change table in his bedroom where you are expected to replace his overburdened diaper. As you pass by the living room, you see Carlos sitting at one of the sofas, appearing sullen while holding a glass of Ann's famous holiday punch (and how anyone can feel sullen while enjoying a glass of Ann's famous holiday punch is beyond you). The recipe is deceptively simple and yet entirely top-secret: 7-Up (the original recipe called for ginger ale, but you would not let her use anything but the best soda around), Tropicana orange juice, Ocean Spray frozen cranberries (not only do they add some festive tartness, they also keep the drink cool without ice cubes diluting the mixture), and a *very* naughty pour of vodka (whatever was on sale at the liquor store). Carlos appears haggard and tired, acknowledging your presence with a quick nod and a mumbled, "Hey." His clothes are wrinkled, his shirt untucked, perhaps even stained. The Carlos of yesteryear would have never made an appearance like this. He was suave and sophisticated. The wild nights you two used to have together when back in the military were legendary. Now, his hair is unkempt, as if he'd only recently rolled out of bed. No matter how many years it has been since his accident, you find it hard to see what this man has become. Understandable, of course, but difficult.

"Hey," you say back with an identical nod and wave.

"Merry Christmas," he says with a tone that might be sarcastic. You can't tell with certainty.

"Merry Christmas."

"I had a poop."

That was Liam, who stands at the top of the stairs, bobbing up and down excitedly, the lowest reaches of his diaper bouncing between each knee. "I know," you reply. Before ascending this last flight, you see that Ann is in the kitchen, standing beside the stove while a frying pan sizzles. She is listening to the quiet words of another person—a man with dark, slicked-back hair and dressed in an immaculate white suit. He turns to reveal his olive skin, trim salt-and-pepper beard, and wide smile. He, too, is imbibing in a glass of Ann's famous holiday punch.

"Hey," Ann says when she notices you standing at the bottom of the stairs. She seems disappointed that you are lingering. "This is Ricardo."

You walk towards him to shake his hand. His grip is strong and confident. "Nice to meet you."

"Nice to meet you, as well." he says with a vague accent that you can't quite put your finger on. Something Latin-based, you assume, wondering if Carlos might be able to identify it. "I have heard a lot about you."

"Have you?" You say, pretending to be bashful, presuming that Ann filled him in on your many years as a fighter-jet pilot, risking your life to keep not only America safe and secure, but also the entire world-order. "What has Ann told you?"

"That you are her husband."

"Oh."

"And that you are a commercial pilot for a mid-sized airline that specializes in short-haul flights across the American Mid-West."

"That is me." Although not what you initially expected, you cannot deny that his brief appraisal of your character is an accurate one. "But I don't think I've heard anything about you. How do you know Ann?"

"We went to college together."

"That's funny. I don't recall Ann ever talking about you."

"Well," Ricardo looks to Ann and shrugs. "I guess there really wasn't much to say. After college, we went our separate ways and only email each other every now and then. I was just in town for the week and she invited me over."

"Where do you live?"

"For the better part of the last ten years, I was living '*off-the-grid*,' you might say, on the island of Hawai'i. I've recently moved back to the continent and am driving across the country, searching for a new place to call home."

"That must be your Audi outside?"

"Yes. It is not an entirely practical car, but I have an affinity for the finer things in life, if you know what I mean." Right as he says this, he looks towards Ann, his expression hidden from you.

"I do know what you mean," you say, holding up the box of 7-Up. "Just saw this at the grocery store. Limited edition Cranberry flavor. Sounds perfect for the holidays." You place it on the kitchen island and look towards Ann. "I figured you could use this in your famous holiday punch."

"I already made it," she says and holds up her glass to make a point.

"I know. But I'm sure you'll need to make a second batch. Three, if the party is a hit."

"I bought the big bottles of 7-Up just for that reason. It would be a waste using cans for a punch, don't you think?"

She does have a point. The purpose of purchasing cans is to enjoy the refreshing, sparkling taste of 7-Up in small doses without the rest going flat. "I guess you are right. I didn't really think about it."

"But I'm sure it will not go to waste," Ricardo says to you.

"Oh, of course not. It's really a perfect drink for the holiday season."

"It is."

"I'd be tempted to have one right now if they were cold."

Ricardo assures: "And I would have one with you."

"Perhaps I should put them in the fridge right now?"

"The sooner, the better."

You open the fridge and sigh. "Darn it."

"What is wrong?" he asks.

"The fridge is full."

"Ah, of course."

"I guess I'll just have to wait."

"Or you could pour a can over ice?" Ricardo says.

"Good idea."

"I had a poop."

Again, that was Liam, presumably still at the top of the stairs, surely straddling a strained sack of effluence. Sadly, there will not be time for a glass of Cranberry 7-Up at this moment. "I'm coming."

Ann says, "You should really go change that diaper right now."

"I will. Nice to meet you, Ricardo. I'm sure we'll talk more."

"Nice to meet you," he stalls and smiles, "too."

Once again, it seems that someone has forgotten your name. But there is no time to press him on the matter. Ann is glaring at you, impatient for you to complete your duties, and you leave the groceries on the kitchen counter to ascend the stairs towards Liam. He raises both arms as you approach, expectant that you will carry him those last few feet. And although he is fully capable of walking, you abide in his request, somehow surprised by his weight even though you are forced to do this on a daily basis. As he lies back on the change table, he reaches back and puts both his hands against his hair, his expression one of unworried calm. When Liam was a baby, he used to resist having his diaper changed, wailing each time as if being mauled, but now this seems to be an experience that he savors. He rests his knees down on their sides to aide in a quick removal of the disposable garment. The seams at the crinkled edge of the diaper, where it meets Liam's clammy upper thighs, are now exposed and forebodingly dark. You know what this means. After unsticking one tab, you pause before pulling back the other, no part of you keen to discover what is about to be revealed.

"Daddy," Liam asks.

"Yes, Liam?"

"Why you waiting?"

"I'm just. Nothing." You pull the other tab and unfold the diaper. Liam's fecal matter appears to have been ejected in two stages. The first is lacking in much viscosity and fills the base of the diaper with a speckled sludge, surely the result of the excessive number of black beans that he consumed at dinner just the previous night. The second stage of this bowel movement is hazel in color, much more solid and formed into a mound to match the contours of his buttocks.

"Daddy," Liam asks.

"Yes, Liam?"

"That's a stinky one!"

"It is."

He tries to prop himself up on each elbow. "What's it look like?"

"It looks like poop, Liam."

He strains to peer over his belly and excitedly adds, "It looks like a volcano!"

Although your son's fidgeting movements are making it difficult to clean his soiled crotch, you must admit that his choice of words are apt. The solid mound of feces does share many similarities in form with a volcano, right down to its caldera peak. And while you are impressed with his metaphor (or is that a simile?), any sense of pride is greatly outweighed by your shame in fathering a three-year-old boy who is still in diapers. Really, once a child has acquired the language to make such figures of speech, shouldn't he be able to use a toilet?

"Daddy?"

"Yes, Liam?"

"It looks like a volcano!"

"I know, Liam."

"A poop volcano!"

"Yes, Liam."

The wrinkles of his scrotum are a dark chestnut, each recession filled with feces. His penis resembles a filthy bishop piece from a chess set, covered in what appears to be specs of muddy sand. For a moment, you stand motionless, surveying the carnage, unsure where to start, delaying the inevitable. How strange it is, you think, that you are so comfortable with staring at a young boy's soiled genitals. Before having children, the thought of this would have been abhorrent. Now, it is part of your procrastination. Because, in a moment, you are going to have to get in there with your hands and clean it up.

"Daddy?"

"Yes, Liam?"

"Are those poo crumbs?"

"What are you talking about, Liam?"

"On my benis? Are those poo crumbs?"

"I'm not sure what that is."

"I think it's poo crumbs."

"Then I guess it's poo crumbs."

"Daddy?"

"Yes, Liam?"

"What are poo crumbs?"

"I don't know, Liam."

"Then how come they are poo crumbs?"

"Because you said they are poo crumbs."

"Daddy?"

"Yes, Liam."

"How did I get poo crumbs on my benis?"

"It's pronounced, '*penis.*'"

"I know."

"You keep saying, 'benis.'"

"I like benis better."

"Okay then," you say, as if to accept his answer, when in actuality his disregard for established pronunciation bothers you. A person cannot simply choose his or her own way of saying any word. The basis of language is that there is a common standard that all speakers accept. You are pondering whether there might be anything to gain by pressing this matter further when Liam asks you another question.

"Daddy?"

"Yes, Liam?"

"Wipe my bum."

"I'm getting started." The sooner you get this over with, the sooner you can go downstairs and enjoy a glass of Ann's famous holiday punch. You reach over towards the wet-wipe warmer (another lavish and ridiculous invention that is likely giving Liam yet more disincentives to move on from diapers) and remember that you were instructed to purchase more wet-wipes from the grocery store. You pop the lid open and see a ruffled, moist tissue folded over. What is impossible to tell, however, is the volume of tissues below. Although you have doubts as to the long-term effectiveness of using wet-wipes, you also know that this particular job would be much more difficult to complete with regular toilet paper. You tug the wipe from its dispenser and another is drawn out through the opening. You pull up Liam's legs by the ankles to start your first pass at the very rear of his buttocks, almost up to your son's lower back. A single, smooth wipe traces a clean line along the boy's skin and renders that particular wipe useless for another pass. You fold it up, place it atop the volcano of poop in the diaper, and pull another wipe from the dispenser.

It is the last one.

"Shoot," you say.

"Daddy?"

"Yes, Liam."

"What's wrong?"

"I'm just out of wet-wipes."

Liam's eyes wince shut. He looks to be in pain and scowls. He then begins to cry.

"Liam, what's wrong?"

"Now my benis is always going to have poo crumbs!"

"No, no, no, no. I'll still be able to clean your benis—I mean your penis."

As quickly as Liam was on the verge of a complete breakdown, he is now calm. "Yay, Daddy!"

Okay. You have just one wipe left. You will need to make the most of it. You decide to go after the scrotum and penis, knowing that the recesses within those folds of skin will make using regular toilet paper extraordinarily difficult. Unfortunately, this is also the part you hate the most. When Emma was a baby, her soiled vagina never seemed to store as much fecal matter as does Liam's genitals— although you also wonder if this is simply due to you having a personal and intimate knowledge of a male's anatomy, whereas the female genitalia continue to be a breeding ground for mystery, even at your age. There is a very real possibility that you rarely cleaned Emma's vagina properly. But she turned out just fine. Perhaps it's not such a big deal, after all?

You have to bat at your son's penis to try and shake off those poo-crumbs, which stick to the foreskin as if covered in honey. Each time you do this, you expect Liam to grumble in pain, but he simply stares up to the spackled ceiling with an appeased smile. There are a couple of specs that will require someone to pick them right off from his skin with a delicate pinch, but that someone is not you. You fold the final wipe onto the diaper.

"Daddy?"

"Yes, Liam."

"Did you get the poo crumbs?"

"I did, Liam."

He reaches down to grab his penis and you swat away his hand.

"Don't touch, Liam. It's dirty down there."

He withdraws his hand and again runs his fingers through his hair. Until having your own children, you never appreciated just how truly and completely disgusting they are. But there is still much left to be cleaned. "Okay, Liam. I've got some good news for you."

"Santa?"

"What? No. This has nothing to do with Santa. This has to do with you becoming a big boy. I'm going to get some toilet paper to finish cleaning you. That's what Daddy, Mommy and Emma all use when we go to the potty. Doesn't that sound like fun?"

Liam's expression is one of tepid fear.

"Okay," you say. "Stay there. I'll be back in a second." You hurry out of the room and continue across the hall towards the bathroom. From down the stairs you can hear Ann welcoming someone at the door. You also hear the sweet sounds of *Wonderful Christmastime* playing on the satellite radio. There is no way you'll be finished changing Liam's diaper before the track is over, and although tempted to linger in the hallway for just a moment to relish in the festive melody, you know that you cannot leave Liam alone for much longer. Inside the bathroom, you pull open the drawer beneath the sink to reveal an array of plump rolls of two-ply toilet paper. Thank you, Costco. Plucking one from the front, you hurry back into Liam's room and find him holding onto his penis once again.

"Liam! Get your hands out of there."

He puts his hands back into his hair and appears to use the wispy strands to clean his fingers. Unfortunately, there is no way that anyone is going to wash him tonight, considering that guests will be over until well past his bedtime, which means you'll have to ensure that you refrain from any needless physical contact with your son until he can be bathed. But when will that be? Surely not on Christmas morning. He will demand opening his presents as soon as possible and then require the rest of the morning to gallivant around the house with his new toys (whatever they are; to be honest, you're really not sure what Ann bought for him this year). Maybe in the afternoon? Perhaps not until after turkey dinner? It could easily be another 24 hours until those poo-crumbs are washed from his hair.

"So, now it's time to be a big boy," you say, holding up the roll of toilet paper.

"Is that going to hurt?"

"No." You're actually not sure. After a lifetime of pre-warmed, pre-moistened towelettes, there is every chance that even the finest two-ply toilet paper will cause discomfort. You wind a tight wad around the fingers of your right hand, tear it off, and take on your son's soiled anus, wiping slowly. He flinches and mutters a quick moan, which coincides with a tightening and then release of his sphincter muscle, creating the impression that it was his anus that groaned. "How was that?" You ask.

"Good."

Good. A curious reply, you think, and one that only seems to validate your fears that Liam is perfectly capable of using a toilet and yet has become too accustomed to this luxuriant service. You unwind another few feet and continue on the other buttocks, this time pushing harder and eliciting an, "Owy," from the boy. You apologize, although in all honesty you are not at all sorry.

"Just a little bit more," you say while wiping the perineal region between his anus and the base of his testicles, curious about that ridge of skin that connects the two, a seam between the boy's left and right sides. You recall being surprised the first time you saw this on Liam, mere hours after his birth, unsure if this was something that all human male's shared. Although you had tried inspecting this on your own body, you fail to have the flexibility to determine this.

"Daddy?"

"Yes, Liam?"

"You think it was the cookies?"

"What's that, Liam?"

"The poo crumbs."

You have no idea what Liam is talking about. "Sorry?"

Now Liam seems annoyed with your confusion and replies impatiently, almost patronizing: "On my benis."

"I know about the poo crumbs on your penis." You really don't feel entirely comfortable saying the word *penis* to your three-year-old son so many times. In fact, you doubt you'll ever feel comfortable saying the word penis to your son (or daughter, for that matter) regardless of his age. Maybe it would be better to say, "benis"?

"I think it's from the cookies."

"Why's that?"

"Because cookies make crumbs. So, cookies should make poo crumbs."

"That could be."

"So, you think Santa will have poo crumbs on his benis?"

"I doubt Santa uses a diaper."

"Oh, yeah."

Here it is: the teachable moment! You feel that this could prove to be the turning point in Liam's toilet training. "You know, Liam, if you started using the potty, then you wouldn't have poo crumbs, either. Just like Santa."

"I like poo crumbs on my benis."

It is a struggle to resist an open sigh. "Oh. Well," you are not sure what else there is to say. Surveying your son's once-soiled nether regions, you feel satisfied with your cleaning. You fold the diaper together and are surprised by its mass as you dispose of it in the over-priced diaper garbage. Liam sits up with his arms outstretched, expecting to be lowered to the carpet. He is wearing nothing but a shirt. "I still have to put a new diaper on you, Liam."

"Oh, yeah."

You grab a diaper from the box beside the change table. Just behind Liam's left foot is a drawer with dozens of unsoiled, unused pairs of underwear, all awaiting his progression from diapers. After a moment of deliberation, you pull open the drawer. "Actually, Liam, I think you are ready to wear a pair of real undies." You hold up one emblazoned with colorful silhouettes of dinosaurs. "Look at this one," you say, attempting to be enthusiastic. "It has dinosaurs."

Liam shakes his head. "I want a diaper."

"You sure?"

He nods, impatient to be returned to the party. There is no more fighting the inevitable. You put on his new diaper, find a pair of pants for him to wear (wondering why Ann ever let him run around the house with just a shirt and diaper in front of the guests) and send him on his way. As you leave the room and head towards the bathroom to wash your hands, you hear Michael Bolton's soulful take on *White Christmas* play from the living room, meaning that *Wonderful Christmastime* has already finished. All you can do is sigh, accept the situation, wash your hands, and then have a glass of Ann's famous holiday punch. That makes everything better.

* * *

The party is a hit. Or, at least it is sufficiently attended to maintain a consistent murmur of conversation. After you ladle your fifth (or is it your sixth?) glass of Ann's famous holiday punch, you collect a few more Triscuits, smear each with a generous helping of Philadelphia Cream Cheese and then top them with a dollop of chili pepper jelly. As you bite into the crispy, creamy, cheesy and oh-so-slightly-spicy snack, you survey what is left of the evening's appetizers. Both the shrimp ring and the ranch and caramelized-onion cheese-ball have long been vanquished. A mere pair of twisted and broken parsnip wedges remain on their Corningware dish and the only evidence of what was once a heaping plate of oven-baked chicken wings is a single, emaciated drumette in a shallow pond of tangerine fat. The tray of meatballs has been reduced to puddles of grease and stray toothpicks, while beads of melted Cracker Barrel cheddar cheese and shriveled bacon bits trace the outline of where there were once potato skins. Of course, the vegetable platter is still stocked with numerous stalks of celery, several stray baby carrots and a half-dozen limp tufts of cauliflower. There are a few oatmeal raisin cookies left, but you recently observed Liam manhandling them with his unsanitary fingers, so there is no way that you're going to eat one now. You lament not having a few different appetizers. A spring roll would have been delicious. Not those limp, refrigerated and supposedly healthy ones that Ann likes to purchase for lunch—you want the crispy, golden deep-fried variety. Or are they called egg rolls? Or are they one and the same? You look around for Ann, planning on telling/asking her about this, but you are not sure where she is.

"Hey, buddy." A hand slaps one shoulder. Turning around (and nearly spilling some of your drink), you see that it is a neighbor from up the street, the one who lives in the rose-colored house with the two-car garage, ornamental front porch, and semi-neglected evergreen tree (which currently has oversized ornaments hanging from its drooping branches; a nice touch, you always think, until he leaves them up well into the month of February). There is always a Ford Escape and Toyota Camry parked on his driveway, causing you to suspect that the garage is essentially used as a place for storage. Unfortunately, this is all you know about this man. You believe he has a wife and at least two children, although you can't be certain. He might be divorced. He could have a cat, and if he does, it's probably that tabby you see wandering through people's front yards. Or maybe his was the one struck by a car last year? The one that no one dared touch for days?

"Hey, buddy." You say in reply.

"Great party." He holds up his glass of Ann's famous holiday punch.

You clang your own glass against his. "Yeah. Thanks."

"Merry Christmas."

"Merry Christmas."

"I could drink these all night." He takes another sip and releases a refreshing sigh. "I'll have to get the recipe from you."

"Well, I could tell you, but then—"

"—You'd have to kill me, right?" He laughs and slaps your shoulder again. "I know, I know."

While you don't appreciate this man appropriating your punchline, you are pleased that he seems to find it humorous. Nothing is exchanged as you stand side-by-side, sipping from your drinks, nodding to the beat of the music (Mariah Carey's seminal *All I Want for Christmas is You*) and watching the mingling, slightly sluggish crowd. You expect this man to ask you another question, but he seems content to say nothing. You, on the other hand, are anything but content with this: "Any plans for the holidays?"

He shrugs, "Ah, just the usual. You know?"

You don't have a clue as to what he means, but still nod in agreement. "Yeah."

"How about you?"

"Same thing. Eat too much. Drink too much."

He chuckles again and holds his glass towards you to initiate another cheers. "I hear you."

"Yeah."

He again makes no attempt to keep the conversation going and yet also makes no attempt to move on to another location in the open-concept living room/kitchen area. Instead, he stands so close that his shoulder just barely rubs against yours every few seconds. You would like to walk away from this man—in fact, you're not even sure if he was invited to this party—but you also don't want to seem rude. You glance back towards him. He smiles, seems ready to ask something, but then takes another sip.

You say, "These go down too quickly."

"Ain't that the truth."

That's it. He says nothing more. You want to ask him about his kids, but you're not sure if he has children. But then you figure that he must—how could any middle-aged man live in this neighborhood and not have children? It's a risky proposition; if he is childless, then this would be an admission of your ignorance.

"Say," you turn towards him. "How old are your kids again?"

"Eight and five." He says and you exhale in relief. "How about you?"

"My son is three, and my daughter is nine, but going on—"

"—Going on fifteen, right?"

You were going to say sixteen, but the gist of the matter seems to have been figured out. "Yeah."

He laughs again, patting your shoulder. "Tell me about it."

You expect him to go into more detail, but instead he appears to wait for you to elaborate. Is he *that* literal? You really don't want to get into it. "Yeah."

"Yeah."

He takes another sip of his drink. "Mmm. These go down too quickly."

"Ain't that the truth," you say.

"Think it's going to snow tonight?"

Although you do not share the general public's affinity for a white Christmas (due to the realities of public aviation during the busy holiday season) you are pleased that this man appears to be making an effort to keep a casual conversation afloat. "Last I checked, the forecast called for a fifty percent probability of precipitation."

He says, "Wouldn't that make the kids happy? Waking up on Christmas morning with a fresh snowfall outside?"

"Yeah," you reply, feeling quite sure that although Liam would be excited, Emma wouldn't really care. You think of relaying this to the man, but don't want to sound rude, so you leave it at that.

He takes another sip of his drink, expels a gratified sigh, but says nothing. This is when you realize that the ball of conversation is now in your court. He attempted to get something going with the talk of snowfall and you ended it with a monosyllabic, "Yeah." You struggle with what you can say, not knowing the man's profession, interests, or name. You take a sip from your glass of Ann's famous holiday punch. "These go down too quickly."

"Ain't that the truth."

You notice that his drink is nearly finished and ponder asking him if he wants a refill, but refrain from doing this, fearing that this might imply a strong desire to continue conversing, or that you want to get him inebriated so that you can take advantage of him. This last theory seems improbable, but it is not a risk that you are willing to take. Instead, you decide to go for the age-old standby: "Seen the price of gas this week?"

"Yeah," he says while shaking his head. "Crazy how much it goes up."

"Always right before a holiday."

"Yup."

"And then takes forever to go down."

The man huffs, still shaking his head, but declines to add more. Now you are really annoyed. He could have complained about taxes. He could have mentioned how cheap gasoline was in another state. He could have referenced the price he paid at some random location this morning. He could have insisted that the oil companies are colluding to keep the prices high. He could have at least blamed the government for doing nothing... but no. He takes another sip of his drink and a once-floating cranberry rolls down to his lips. He then says, "These go down too quickly."

"Ain't that the truth."

"Think I might get a refill. You want a top-up?"

Your glass is less than half-full, but you decline his offer with a gentle shake of your head. "Nah, I'm okay."

"Come on, it's not like you have to drive, right?"

"Well then, okay." You hold out your glass and this man ladles in another scoop of Ann's famous holiday punch. The two of you clang your drinks together again, take synchronized sips, and then stand with your backs to the table staring out. You feel trapped, burdened by a full glass of punch that forces you to stay with him for at least another few minutes. But what else is there to ask? Christmas plans, children, the weather and even the price of gasoline have already been exhausted. You definitely do not want to bring up politics—that always gets far too dire and serious these days. You could say that you have to go to the restroom, but that might seem too obvious. You can't be the rude one. You are the co-host of this appie party.

You take another sip of your drink and say, "These go down far too quickly."

"Say," he says to you. "You were in the Air Force, right?"

"Yeah," you reply, taken aback by his knowledge of your past. You don't even know his name. But clearly your reputation precedes you. "How did you know?"

"I was talking to that guy over there. The moody looking one." He points towards Carlos, who sits alone at one end of a sofa, staring at the Christmas tree, talking with no one. "He said you two served together."

"Well, not to brag, but I was once one of the elite—among the most skilled and respected, if not feared, fighter pilots in the American Air Force. The F-22 Raptor, the F-177 Nighthawk and even the—"

"—Cool, cool." He says, interrupting you, seemingly impatient. "That's what I heard. Anyhow, I was just wondering if I could ask you a question about your time there, if you don't mind?"

You can only guess what he is going to query you on. There are so many amazing stories. The time you were shot down over

Afghanistan and had to hide in mountainous caves for weeks until being rescued. How you were there the day Saddam Hussein's statue was toppled in Firdos Square, cheering on with the newly (albeit, perhaps temporarily) liberated people of Baghdad. Maybe Carlos told him about that long weekend in Tijuana with Caliente, your favorite masseuse/prostitute at that time? "Ask anything. I mean," you look over both shoulders. "Anything, assuming that my wife isn't listening, right?"

He forces out a chuckle and slaps your shoulder again. "I know what you mean, buddy. Anyhow, I was just thinking. When you were on missions, you'd be up in the air for hours at a time, right?"

"Easily two or three, yes."

"Well, there must be times that you have to, you know, relieve yourself?"

"Usually, we try to do that before we take off."

"But, you know, there must be times when you can't help yourself, right?"

You begrudgingly nod. "Yes."

"So, what do you do then? There can't be toilets on a fighter jet, can there?"

"No, of course not." This is not what you wanted to talk about. There must be literally *hundreds* of interesting stories that you could tell this man about. Granted, the vast majority of those are classified, but even then, you figure there must be at least a dozen anecdotes that the general public may be privy to.

"So?"

"Well, there is something called a piddle bag."

"A piddle bag?"

"Yeah. It's essentially a catheter tube that leads into a polyethylene storage vessel."

"So, you stick a straw up your Johnson and then pee into a plastic baggie?"

His layman's description of the procedure is sound. "Yes."

"Isn't that ironic? You're up there, surrounded by some of the most advanced technology in the world, but when nature calls, it all comes down to a straw and a Ziplock bag."

"It's called a piddle bag, and it's not a Ziplock—"

He slaps your shoulder again. "Anyhow, buddy, it's time for me to use the restroom. That is, unless you have one of those piddle bags around here?"

"No. I do not."

"I was just kidding you." He takes back what is almost an entire glass of Ann's famous holiday punch in a single, drawn-out gulp. "These go down far too quickly." He places his empty cup on the table behind you.

"Ain't that the truth," you say as he walks away, unsure if he was attempting to demean your role in the world's most powerful military. If this is the case, then his mission was an unqualified failure. You would like to see that man (whatever his name is) sit in a confined cockpit for three hours, unclip his seat belts, unzip his flight suit and use that piddle bag all without making a mess. Either way, you are relieved that he has exited your immediate surroundings and decide to seek out Carlos. Although you still consider him one of your best friends, it has been a challenge to have a casual conversation with him of late. Ever since his accident, he hasn't been the same man, and you've generally found it easier to neglect making contact with him, rather than struggle with finding things to talk about. But he's sitting all alone and you can ask him about that man with the bizarre interest in piddle bags. That should buy you at least a couple of minutes of small talk, enough to keep you from feeling like you're being a poor host and/or friend.

Carlos leans against the armrest of a sofa adjacent to the Christmas tree, staring at the strands of white lights with an expression as empty as a checking account after New Year's Day. As you approach, you hold up your glass of Ann's famous holiday punch, intending to partake in a festive *cheers*, but then notice that he doesn't even have a beverage. "Where is your drink?" you ask.

"I've already had a few. I need to drive."

"They are delicious, aren't they?"

"They sure are," he says, his tone unconvincing.

"It's Ann's specialty."

"I know."

"People call it: *Ann's famous holiday punch.*"

"Do they?"

"Yeah." You shrug. "Some people."

"Like who?"

"I do."

Carlos nods. "Oh yeah."

"You want something else? I can offer you some 7-Up."

"No, thanks."

"Actually," you snap your fingers, "I have a great idea. Wait here." You turn, ready to hurry away.

"No, no, no. I'm okay. Promise."

"But you don't know what I'm going to get you."

"Is it that Cranberry 7-Up?"

How did he know? And regardless of how he was able to guess this with such confidence, there is an even more pressing question: why does he still turn down the offer? "It is."

"You already told me about that 12-pack you picked up."

"I did?"

"Yeah. Right after you changed your son's diaper."

"Oh yeah."

"But thanks for the offer."

"Have you had one yet?"

"No."

"Then I should get you one."

"I don't really feel like a soda. Too sweet."

"I think you might find that the tartness of the cranberry nicely compliments the high-fructose corn syrup."

"I think I'll be okay. Thanks."

"It's limited edition. You never really know how long it's going to be around for."

"I'm okay."

"It wouldn't be a problem for me to grab one. I promise."

Carlos represses a groan. He says, almost forcefully: "And I promise that I don't want a soda. But thanks, *again*, for the offer."

You hold up one hand and nod in acknowledgement. "I can take a hint."

Carlos chuckles to himself.

"Do you want a glass of water?"

"No thanks."

"Or we have bottles of both Aquafina and Dasani. Ann is more of a Dasani woman, but I'm an Aquafina man all the way."

"I'm good."

"Okay, then. Just thought I'd offer."

"I can see that."

You have this nagging thought that Carlos would rather you leave him alone. You've felt this before at other occasions, but upon any amount of contemplation, you always come to the same conclusion—of course he's grateful to have you around. After all, he is the moody and difficult one, while you are pleasant and agreeable to all people. What, at times, you mistake as annoyance is just part of his overall demeanor, an unpleasant consequence of his recovery from the incident.

"Hey," you then remember why you came over here in the first place. "I was just talking to this guy a few minutes ago. Said he spoke to you about our time in the Air Force."

"Oh yeah, I remember him."

You expect him to say more on the matter.

He does not say more on the matter.

You say, "Weird guy, right?"

"How so?"

"I don't know." You shrug, figuring that it was obvious. "Just kind of hard to talk to."

"He seemed about as easy to talk to as anyone else."

"Really?"

"Yeah."

"Huh." You then add, "Had a strange interest in how we'd relieve ourselves while in flight."

"I guess it's a fair question. Not like there are going to be toilets on an F-16."

"True. I just figured, if you're going to ask a pilot about his time in the Air Force, there are so many more interesting things to ask about."

"I don't know," Carlos shrugs, staring at the tree. "What one person finds interesting, another person finds boring." He then looks at you. "Really boring."

"True." You say with a nod, knowing exactly what he means. People like you and Carlos have lived a very different life compared to the vast majority of the human race. Most can't even fathom the events that you have experienced.

Just then, you notice the song playing over the satellite radio. *Wonderful Christmastime* by The Beatles. It's a Christmas miracle! You wouldn't have thought that you would have had the chance to hear it again in the same evening. "Ah, I love this song."

"I know."

"It's definitely my favorite Beatles song, and might be my favorite Christmas song, as well."

Carlos sighs. "We've gone through this before. It's not a Beatles song."

"Yes it is."

"It's a Paul McCartney song."

"No, it's not."

"Yes, it is. I can Google it right now just to prove it to you," Carlos says, seemingly ready to take out his phone.

Wouldn't that be a petty move, you think, and one that feels utterly in contrast to what the Christmas spirit is all about. "No, that's all right."

"So, you believe me?"

"No. I just don't think we need to do that."

"The song was released, like, ten years after The Beatles broke up."

You ask, "You know who I wished released a Christmas song?"

Carlos answers: "Chumbawamba."

"Have I told you that before?"

"Just about every Christmas."

"Really?"

"Yeah."

"That can't be true."

"Then how else would I know?"

That seems like a silly question. "Because Chumbawamba is one of my favorite bands."

Carlos nearly scoffs and asks, "What albums do they have?"

"Well, *Tubthumping,* of course."

"Was that the name of the song or the name of the album?"

"I'm pretty sure it's the same thing."

"Okay, then, what other albums do they have?"

"I don't really know."

"Then how can they be one of your favorite bands if you don't even know the name of one other album?"

"Why does that matter?"

"Because if Chumbawamba is really one of your favorite bands, then you should be able to mention the name of at least one other album."

Even by Carlos' standards, he is in a cranky mood. But you're not about to let this go as easily as your debate regarding *Wonderful Christmastime*. He is, after all, questioning your passion for the one-and-only Chumbawamba. "But I don't think any of their other albums are as good as Tubthumping."

"Well, that settles it, then. You can't call Chumbawamba one of your favorite bands."

"Of course I can."

"Tell me another song they do, besides *Tubthumper*."

"It's *Tubthumping*."

"Whatever."

"Well," you pause to think. You recall your old CD with the album. Chumbawamba was quite helpful in putting *Tubthumping* first in the track order. You never had to bother paying attention to any of the other tracks or their numbers. "I can't really remember."

"Because that's the only song you listened to."

"Because it's such a great song."

"One song shouldn't make them one of your favorite bands."

"Depends how good the song is." You then pause and a horrible thought surfaces. "Wait, don't you like the song?"

"It is what it is."

"It's a great song."

"Sure."

"Did I tell you about the time I was on hold and *Tubthumping* played, like, ten times in a row?"

"You have told me that."

"So, obviously I'm not the only one who likes Chumbawamba. Right?"

Carlos shakes his head. "I can't believe I've been talking about Chumbawamba for the last ten minutes."

"It wasn't ten minutes," you say. "Probably just one or two."

"And I can't believe I've said *Chumbawamba* so many times."

"It's a fun name to say. Feels good." You take another sip from your glass of Ann's famous holiday punch and realize that it's nearly empty. "Say, I'm going to top this up. You sure you don't want one?"

"I'm good. Thanks."

"And the offer still stands on a Cranberry 7-Up."

"No thanks."

"Or an Aquafina?"

"I'm good."

"Dasani?"

"No, thanks."

"Your loss," you say with a sly grin before standing up and walking back towards the kitchen island. As you refill your cup, you notice that the punch hardly even fizzles anymore, which is not at all surprising considering that this current batch has been sitting out on the counter for over an hour. You find it interesting how you would never enjoy a can of flat, room-temperature soda, but a glass of flat, room-temperature punch (well, Ann's *famous* holiday punch) is just fine.

"Dad," you hear a girl call from behind. It's Emma, and she's clearly disgruntled. She holds up her iPad. "Liam keeps bugging me, trying to take this away."

"Shouldn't he be in bed by now?"

"He keeps getting out."

You sigh, figuring that this really should be Ann's responsibility. "Where is your mother?"

"I don't know. I couldn't find her. But can you do something about this?"

Of course you can. You just don't want to. It's past ten in the evening and one shouldn't be dealing with offspring at this time.

"Can't you just tell him to go back to sleep? Maybe tell him that Santa won't give him any presents if he keeps getting out."

"Why don't you do that?"

"I'm in the middle of something."

"Of what?"

Drinking. "I'm having a grown-up conversation with Uncle Carlos over there. He's expecting me back any second now."

"It's not fair that he keeps getting out of his room."

"Well," you sigh, "Why don't you take the iPad to the bathroom and lock the door? Then he can't get in."

She seems surprised, maybe even mildly repulsed. "Really?"

You thought that it was a pretty good idea, considering that you had limited time to think. "Really. And I'll go talk to Liam in a minute."

"Promise?"

No, you won't. "Of course. Now, go."

Emma shakes her head as she walks away and up the stairs. You chuckle while returning to Carlos, who passes you a limp smile as you take a seat beside him. "Sorry about that," you say.

"About what?"

"About taking so long."

"Oh. I didn't really notice."

"I got held up by Emma."

"Oh yeah."

"I tell you, she may be nine years old, but she's going on sixteen."

Carlos doesn't reply or react. He seems frozen in time. He must have not heard you. And fair enough—the boisterous Jackson 5 rendition of *I Saw Mommy Kissing Santa Claus* is playing especially loud. You repeat yourself: "I tell you, she's like nine going on sixteen."

"Yeah, I heard."

You can't blame Carlos for not finding great humor in this joke.

He chose not to have children and will hence never fully appreciate the full breadth of the human condition. Well, perhaps it is a bit harsh to say that he *chose* to not have children. Due to his accident, he is incapable of producing offspring. But, until the day of that incident, it was a choice. And considering that he is 45 years old, and that his accident occurred almost five years ago, then that means about 90% of the cause for his childlessness can be attributed to personal choice.

You then realize: no male human has the ability to produce virile semen until adolescence. This means that Carlos had from the age of 15 through to the age of 40 to impregnate a woman. So, that makes 25 years of possible breeding time out of his 45 years of existence. You take out your phone to use the calculator. Carlos had just over 55% of his time on Earth to procreate, and during that time, it was a matter of his own volition that he remains devoid of progeny. Not 90%, but still substantial.

Carlos says, "You checking who wrote *Wonderful Christmastime?*"

"No," you say with a chuckle. "Just needed to perform a quick calculation."

"I won't be insulted if you check."

"No need, my friend. No need." You then savor a sip of Ann's famous holiday punch and remember something of interest to bring up to Carlos. "So, hey, as I was refilling my glass of Ann's famous holiday punch, I had a realization. Pretty much no one would drink a glass of warm, flat soda. Right?" You pause to give Carlos a moment to think about this and reply.

He seems to wait for you to continue. Then, "Sure."

"So, then why is it that everyone here is so willing to drink up glasses full of Ann's famous holiday punch?"

Again, Carlos doesn't appear to realize that he's been asked a question. He starts to shake his head, almost indifferent. "Because there's booze in it?"

That is a good point. Even though every adult in this room could easily afford to purchase a bottle of liquor, the lure of *free* alcohol entices people to consume it in quantities that far surpass any of the food products. Even those delectable oven-baked parsnip wedges have yet to be entirely consumed—and who doesn't love a good parsnip? "I guess that could be it. Well, that, and that this punch is delicious." You punctuate your statement with another sip from the drink, really wishing that Carlos would imbibe with you. Surely it would lighten his mood. "You certain you don't want even a small glass?"

"I'm very certain."

"You do know that you're missing out, right?"

"I've already had some."

"But it seems like you should have another."

"You've asked me, like, three times already."

"I think just two."

"No, it's been three. At least." Carlos sighs and winces, but then forces a grimaced smile, his expression conciliatory. "I'm sorry. You're just trying to be nice."

He should be sorry and you accept his apology in thought. "No need to be sorry. I do get a little carried away with these things." You are then struck by a pang of *snunger*, a term you coined to describe the sensation of desiring something to snack upon (as if being hungry) while knowing that there is no conceivable way your body actually requires further sustenance. "Say," you turn back to Carlos. "Did you try some of that shrimp from the shrimp ring?"

"I did."

"Great, right?"

"Yeah."

"They really should call it a *king prawn ring*, those shrimp were so big."

"They were."

"And there was something in that dipping sauce that had some kick."

Carlos nods.

You ask, "What do you think that was?"

"Sorry?"

"What do you think made that spiciness?"

"Some spice."

You chuckle. "Good one. But what spice? I'm thinking it might have been cayenne."

"Maybe.

"Speaking of spice, did you have any of that chili pepper jelly?"

"Uh, no."

"You didn't?" You are ready to stand, knowing that there was still some left as of a couple of minutes ago. If Carlos refuses to have any more of Ann's famous holiday punch due to this nanny-state's overbearing impaired driving laws, then he has no reason to turn down an alcohol-free snack. "How about I fix you up a cracker with some right now?"

"Oh, no, thanks. I'm good."

"Do you like genuine Philadelphia Cream Cheese?"

Carlos appears confused, but slowly replies, "Sure."

"And do you like Triscuits?" You feel ridiculous as you say this. Of course he likes Triscuits.

"I guess."

"Well, I tell you, put some cream cheese and chili pepper jelly on a Triscuit, and you're in Flavortown."

Carlos looks disgusted. "Did you just say, Flavortown?"

"Yeah. It's something I say. I made it up."

"No, you didn't."

"I'm pretty sure I did. It's like *snunger.*"

"What is that?"

"Snunger. When you've got the snacking hunger."

"Okay, I think you did make that one up."

"It's pretty good, right?"

Carlos seems to cough out a laugh. "Yeah."

"So," you stand up, "I'll make you one right now."

"No, no, no. I'm good. Trust me. I don't need anything."

"I guess you're not at all *snungry*, are you?"

"What? Oh. No, I'm not."

"Well, if you can show the willpower to resist, then so can I, right?"

"Yeah."

You look back to the kitchen island and make visual confirmation that there are still Triscuits. Why did you tell Carlos that you didn't need a snack in that foolish act of solidarity? Now you can't stop thinking about how snungry you are. Surely just a single loaded Triscuit would quell this desire?

No. You and Carlos went to war together. You risked your lives together. The two of you have endured trauma the likes of which few people in this world can appreciate. You don't need another snack right now, no matter how snungry you feel.

That is, unless, Carlos changes his mind. Then it would be rude to sit back and not partake.

You ask, "Did you try any of those meatballs?"

"I didn't."

"Oh, you should have. They were certified Angus."

"Oh, yeah."

"They were a hit."

"Yeah."

"From Costco."

"Oh, yeah."

"Only, like, ten bucks for that huge tray."

"Yeah."

"Did you see how many meatballs there were?"

"Yeah."

"Ten bucks! I love Costco."

"Oh, yeah."

"It's amazing what you can get from there."

"Yeah."

"Although lately the parking there has been a nightmare."

"Oh, yeah."

"Usually there is ample parking. But lately." You shake your head to visualize your dismay. "Christmas shopping, right?"

"Oh, yeah."

"I go to the one right off the Johnston Hill overpass. It's been just terrible there, lately."

"Yeah."

"How about you? Is that the one you go to?"

"I don't have a Costco membership."

It is impossible to disguise your shock. Next you'll discover that he regularly takes public transit. "What?" You then realize, "Oh, so you're a Sam's Club guy?"

"No. I don't shop there, either."

"Then where do you shop?"

Carlos shrugs, "Stores."

You're about to unload a zinger on Carlos (*"I guess you're just one of those people who like to pay more for less!"*) before realizing that he lives alone and it would be exceptionally difficult for one man to consume the volume of items purchased at a membership-only retail warehouse club. However, you then realize that this could be rectified with a deep freeze and a little bit of planning. *And* there are countless non-perishable items at great prices in a Costco that any man—a lone wolf or part of the pack—can (and should) take advantage of. Although, to be fair, his Jaguar XKR is hardly the most practical vehicle for transporting large quantities of merchandise. Yet another reason why sports cars, as flashy and powerful as they are, fail to surpass the practicality (and safety) of a Volvo sedan.

You then remember something else to mention. "But, you know what's interesting? Went there the other week, and guess what they didn't have?"

"Went where?"

"To Costco."

"Still talking about Costco?"

"Of course! Anyhow, guess what they didn't have?"

Carlos shakes his head.

"No, make a guess." You really don't appreciate it when people give up before making a single attempt.

"Condoms?"

"What?" You then realize that Carlos was making a joke and laugh. Although, as your chuckle winds down, you do wonder if Costco sells contraceptives. Now that you think about it, you've never noticed them anywhere. Not that you'd need them. You had your vasectomy within months of Liam's birth. But is there really anyone out there partaking in sexual intercourse so frequently that he (or she) needs to take advantage of the economies of scale when purchasing prophylactics? You will have to remember to check the next time you visit Costco. "Actually, just today while I was at the grocery store, some teenagers put a pack of condoms into my basket."

"You saw them do it?"

"Well, no. But I knew it was them."

"Oh, yeah."

"So, anyhow, guess what Costco didn't have?"

Carlos sighs, "I don't know."

"You have to make a guess."

"I did."

Although you feel that he is squeaking by on a technicality, you will let this one pass. "Fair enough. What Costco didn't have were any Christmas lights."

"Oh. Yeah."

"Isn't that interesting?"

"Yeah."

"I remember seeing them there in the fall. Maybe back in September, or something. Or maybe even in August. It was early enough for me to think to myself, '*Who buys Christmas lights already?*'" As you finish your sentence, you then realize the answer to this (once) rhetorical question: *Prudent shoppers.*

"Oh, yeah."

"You would think that Costco would sell Christmas lights close to Christmas, but I guess not."

"Yeah."

"Must have something to do with their business model."

"Yeah."

"Which is too bad, because Ann and I had to drive all over the place trying to find lights for a decent price. Which just means trying to find parking at one mall after another."

"Yeah."

"And although I know I said that parking at Costco has been terrible of late, believe me, I'd much rather deal with that than trying to find a spot at a mall these days. Right?"

"Oh, yeah."

"Have you been to Crosstown Mall lately?"

"Yeah."

"Then you know what I mean, right? I was watching the morning news with Darren Wilks and Tina Gables the other day," you then hesitate, unsure if you are remembering these pertinent details correctly. "Or was I watching the morning news with Sophie Chan and Glenn Wilson?" You really can't remember. Both morning shows do an upstanding job relaying the latest global crises and local traffic advisories, as well as broadcasting light-hearted pieces that bring you a much appreciated chuckle during those manic early-morning weekdays. "Who do you prefer?"

"Oh, yeah."

Oh, Carlos. Always a joker. "I bet it's Darren Wilks and Tina Gables, right?"

"Yeah."

"I think it probably was them. They have the Arby's Trafficopter, and I find that having an 'eye-in-the-sky' really helps give them the scoop on vehicular incidents around town."

"Yeah."

"Remember when they called it the Taco Bell Trafficopter? I wonder why Taco Bell gave up the sponsorship? I liked the sound of that better. It must be the alliteration." You then sip from your glass of Ann's famous holiday punch and try to remember what you were talking about. "What was I going to tell you about, again?"

"Oh," Carlos is taken off guard by your question, "I really don't know."

You laugh and hold up your glass of Ann's famous holiday punch. "Too many of these, I guess. Right?'

"Yeah."

You then snap your fingers, startling Carlos. "That's it! I was talking about parking."

"Oh, yeah."

"And I saw this story on the morning news the other day where parking was just a mess at Crosstown Mall and someone called 9-1-1 to complain about it. Can you believe that? A woman calling 9-1-1 just to say that she couldn't get a parking spot?" While recounting this anecdote (or could you call it a vignette?), you realize that there is no way that you can be assured of the offending person's gender. On the news (which you are now 80% certain was with Darren Wilks and Tina Gables) they showed the spokesman for the police reminding people that 9-1-1 calls are for emergencies only, but there was never any audio of the actual phone call. "I tell you, I don't know about some people these days."

"Yeah."

"You know, you and I, we've been to war. We know what a real crisis entails."

"Yeah."

"Speaking of Christmas lights, let me ask you a question." You draw Carlos' attention towards the Christmas tree. "Ann and I got into a bit of a—let's just call it a *debate*—although, let me tell you, it got quite heated. But when we were buying new lights for the tree this year, one of us wanted those ones there. They're called *warm white*." You then point towards a strand of tiny bulbs wound around some garland that drapes over the living room window. "And one of us wanted lights for the tree like those. They're called *icy white*."

"Oh, yeah."

"So, which ones do you prefer?"

Carlos sighs, "Sorry?"

"Which ones do you like better? Not telling you what side I'm on. Do you prefer the warm white or the icy white?"

"They're both good?"

"No, no, no. You have to pick a side. They are quite different, really."

Carlos looks at the tree for hardly a second, then glances towards the garland and shrugs. "I guess, this one?" He motions towards the warm white lights on the Christmas tree.

"Huh," you say, surprised. "That was Ann's pick."

"Sorry."

"No, don't apologize. It's a matter of opinion. Why do you like that one better?"

"I don't know. They're warmer?"

You begrudgingly nod. "That's what Ann said. And I see what

you mean. The lights do have a more classic look, you know? And, obviously, Ann won that argument—or I should say debate—but I always thought the icy white look would be better. It's Christmas, right? What's Christmas without frostiness? Without iciness? Plus we already had that strand around the garland there, so I figured that it would make sense to have a common theme in this space. But what do I know? Ann assumes that just because I'm a man that I don't have any design sense. And don't get me wrong, I think the Christmas tree looks great. Ann prefers the simple, uncluttered look, and I agree with that. I don't like it when it's covered in hundreds of knick-knacks. That's just messy. Makes it look like a hoarder decorated the thing. But, I don't know." You sit back, admiring the tree while savoring another sip of Ann's famous holiday punch. "I still think it could use that icy touch. But you know what they say: happy wife, happy life, right?"

Carlos rubs his face into both palms. He must be exhausted. To be honest, he should have left this party at least an hour ago.

You then say, "I think next year, I'm going to watch for those lights at Costco again. Even if it's summer. I think if I can get a quality strand of icy-whites at a good price, then maybe next Christmas we can try putting them on and I bet once Ann actually sees the tree with the icy-whites, how it will match the garland there with the same icy-whites, then—"

Carlos sits up straight and interrupts. "I'm sorry. I just can't do this anymore."

"What's that?"

He shakes his head, bewildered or in disbelief. "I can't handle this another second. I just. I can't do it."

"Can't do what?"

"You. I can't do *you* for another second. I mean, how much longer can you talk about Christmas lights for? Not even colored ones. Different shades of white. I mean, this is crazy." He stands up, still rubbing his eyes, shaking his head. "You used to be interesting, man. You used to be one of the elite. *You were the Ace of Spades.* What happened? I'm sorry, but I can't be friends with you anymore. You're just too boring. How long can a man talk about Costco for? I don't know, but I'm starting to find out. You can talk about Costco forever! And I can't handle another conversation about 7-Up. I don't even like 7-Up. It tastes like Sprite. It's the same thing with a different name. And if I have to hear you say, '*Ann's famous holiday punch,*' one more time—just one more time—I think I might snap. I might actually kill you. I'm serious. It's for your own best interest that I leave and never, ever, talk to you again. If I don't go right now, it's very likely that I'll commit manslaughter." Carlos' words have now attracted the eavesdropping attention of the others in the room. No one else is saying anything as you remain on the couch and Carlos stands, nearly shaking. Michael Bublé's instant-classic rendition of *It's Beginning to Look A Lot Like Christmas* plays over the speakers and you find it hard not to tap your foot. It's that good. Carlos takes a deep breath and then a single step back. "I'm sorry to say this, but you have to be the most boring person in the entire world."

With that, Carlos walks towards the foyer, but then stops and turns to add: "And Chumbawamba were a one-hit-wonder. And speaking of wonder, *Wonderful Christmastime* is not a Beatles song. Look the damn thing up on your phone." He then shakes his head, annoyed with himself for getting drawn back, and leaves the house.

Nervous glances slowly return to you and your spot on the sofa. You take a sip from your glass of Ann's famous holiday punch and frown as if to apologize, sorry that everyone else had to bear witness to Carlos' outburst. And on Christmas Eve, of all days. "He's disfigured," you say with a prolonged shrug. It really seems to explain everything.

* * *

You are awoken by clomping steps. As your eyes focus, you realize that you are on the living room sofa. Clearly everyone left while you were unconscious. Your glass of Ann's famous holiday punch is still in one hand, and, miraculously, none seems to have spilled. Looking at your phone, you see that it is just past midnight, which means that it is now Christmas Day. You put down your drink and plan on making your way up to your bedroom—and specifically to your Sealy Posturepedic pillow-top mattress—when you notice something amazing.

The Beatles' *Wonderful Christmastime* is playing on the satellite radio for the third time this evening.

"I must be dreaming," you say.

There is then another shuffling step. Assuming it to be Ann, you sit up and look towards the kitchen, expecting her to be gathering up plates and wiping down the many fingerprints on all the stainless steel appliances. But it's not Ann. Standing by the nearly emptied trays of appetizers is a large, rotund (and surely obese, in terms of his body-mass-index) old man in a velvety red coat and matching pants. The trim of his collar and sleeves is a plush, snowy fur. He turns to reveal his great white beard and woolly eyebrows. He's eating one of the leftover oatmeal-raisin cookies and smiles as you make eye contact. "You're awake," he says to you with some food still in his mouth, his voice a hearty baritone. Unbeknownst to him, a few oats fall from his lips and onto the floor.

"Santa?" You say in disbelief, staggering a few steps as you approach him.

"That's me," he holds out a gloved hand. "Merry Christmas."

As you shake his hand, you are surprised both by the strength of his grip, as well as how luxuriously smooth and soft his gloves are. "Merry Christmas," you say.

"These cookies are delicious. Give my best to Ann, will you?"

As he takes another bite, you recall Liam manhandling these exact same biscuits, grabbing one and then putting it back before plucking another. Should you tell him about this? If Santa Claus developed some sort of gastrointestinal distress because of an E. coli infection, the results would be disastrous. Millions, maybe billions, of the world's children would rush to the Christmas tree in the morning only to find a vacant space. Christmas Day would be ruined, all because of your complicit silence.

Although, to be honest, your immediate family would be just fine. Clearly Santa Claus is ready to deliver your presents and any infection would require an incubation period of several hours, *at the very least*. Chances are, he wouldn't notice any symptoms until the following day. So, Christmas would not be ruined. And, considering that this man spends much of his working day in close confines with magical caribou (you refuse to call them reindeer; you don't live in Scandinavia and hence shouldn't be using their parlance), then he is surely in contact, direct or indirect, with animal feces on a regular basis. One would think that such exposure over the years would lead Santa Claus to developing a robust immune system with regards to such pathogens. Really, as unhygienic as Liam can be, he must be immaculate when compared with a caribou? Magical or not, you doubt that Rudolph can wash his own hooves.

But, no. The risks, unlikely as they may be, are unacceptable to you. And although your family would come out unscathed, the spirit of Christmas is about giving, or something. Actually, you're not sure what the spirit of Christmas is about, exactly. Perhaps you should ask Santa? Surely he would know. But regardless of this, it's decided: Santa Claus should stop eating those oatmeal-raisin cookies.

"Actually, Santa," you say, motioning towards the cookie that he'd just taken from the plate, "I hate to say, but I think there might be some of my son's fecal matter on those. He's always putting his hands down around his genitals and he does an atrocious job of washing his hands."

"Ho, ho, ho," Santa bellows. "Do not worry about me. I spend my days with eight reindeer that defecate anywhere they please. Do that for as many years as I have, and you become pretty much immune to any bacterium."

"You know, I was actually thinking about that." You are then struck by one of the things Santa just said. "Wait, did you say eight reindeer? I assumed there were nine."

"No, there needs to be symmetry on the line. Four on each side."

"Makes sense. So, let me try to remember them all." You hold up one hand to start keeping track on your fingers. "There's Dasher and Dancer, Prancer and, oh, what was next?"

Santa smiles but shakes his head. "You can't ask for help that quickly."

"You're right, Santa. You're right. Oh, what was it?" You go back to the beginning, hoping the names follow through naturally. "There's Dasher and Dancer, Prancer and *Vixen*."

"Well done."

"There was a band in the 80's called Vixen. Wasn't there?"

Santa shrugs.

"I think it was an all-female glam metal group. Can't remember any of the names of their hits. They were more of a one-hit-wonder, or at least a novelty. I remember a video of the drummer playing in high heel boots... and I want to say boots with stirrups."

"The only Vixen I know is one heck of a hard working reindeer."

"Fair enough. I'm sure she'd have to be."

"She?" Santa shakes his head. "Vixen is male."

"Huh. I would have thought, from the name, that Vixen would be a girl."

Santa grabs the last remaining oatmeal-raisin cookie with one gloved hand while still chewing another. "No, no, no. All my reindeer are males. You really think a woman can do that much hard work? Ho, ho, ho! That's a good one."

While initially surprised by Santa's chauvinistic attitude, you have to accept that he is a very, very old man. You can only imagine how set in his ways he must be at this age. Although uncertain as to when exactly he started out, it was certainly a long time before the women's liberation movements of the twentieth century. It's actually quite possible that Santa doesn't believe that women should have the right to vote. But, you'll make sure you don't press the matter and doubt that Women's Suffrage will come up in light conversation. "So," you say, "that's four. What's next? *Dasher, Dancer, Prancer, Vixen.* Then, Comet—"

"Oh, Comet is dead."

"Oh," although you feel that you should be saddened to hear this news, you also realize that you don't know the difference between any of Santa's caribou. "I'm sorry to hear that."

"These things happen."

"Can I ask how he passed?"

"Broken leg. Had to put him down."

"Fair enough. Who has he been replaced with?"

"Gary. He's a firecracker, that one."

"So, that makes *Dasher, Dancer, Prancer, Vixen, Gary.* Then, is it Cupid?"

"It is."

"Then Donner and—"

"Actually, Donner died, as well."

"Broken leg?"

"No. A polar bear got him."

"Sheesh. That sounds nasty."

Santa takes a bite of his cookie, appearing indifferent. "It's part of the natural cycle of life up north."

"Who replaced Donner?"

"Donald."

"That's handy."

"Makes it easy to remember, doesn't it?"

"It does." You say, thinking that Comet should have been replaced with a Connor, not Gary. "So, just one left. Back to the start." You clear your throat. "There's Dasher, Dancer, Prancer, Vixen, Gary, Cupid, Donner—I mean *Donald*—and Blixen."

"Well done."

"So, what about Rudolph?"

"Oh, he's just a story popularized by the song. You really believe that a glowing red nose would make any difference when dealing with low visibility situations? You're a pilot, right? A bright light in a dense fog would only illuminate the immediate moisture. It would be useless. Just like you rely on your instruments, I rely on a sense of feel."

"Actually," you admit, "to be honest, these days I pretty much just rely on auto-pilot."

"Actually," Santa admits with a hearty chuckle, "to be honest, these days the reindeer pretty much fly themselves. They've been doing it for so long, I don't really have to do much of anything."

"Can I ask you another question about your caribou?"

"Ask me anything."

"What happens when they defecate in mid-flight? Does it just drop," you leave your question hanging, knowing that Santa gets the gist of your question.

Santa nods and shrugs. "It just drops. Although, at the altitudes that we're flying, it hits the ground as frozen particulate matter, so it's of no harm to anyone."

"You know what's funny? It's amazing how many people think that's what happens on airplanes. They assume that the sucking sound when you flush is the water and waste being sucked out into the low pressure environment of the stratosphere."

"Ho, ho, ho," Santa chuckles again (and with a seeming disregard for the fact that there are others sleeping in the house). "Don't people realize how much waste would be raining down from the heavens? There's only one of me. Imagine how many airplanes must be in the air at any given time? It would be a terrible mess."

"During peak travel hours, there are up to ten thousand planes in flight at once."

Santa seems surprised. "Really? That many?"

"Yeah. In just the United States, there are up to five thousand planes in the air at once."

Santa takes another bite of a cookie and nods to himself. "Well, I guess with over three hundred million people living over a large land mass and a great number of dispersed but integrated employment centers, it makes sense. A typical plane carries, what, one or two hundred passengers?"

This seems like a reasonable estimate—pretty good for an old man who likely has never been on a commercial flight. "Yeah. Maybe more like one hundred and fifty to two hundred."

"So, five thousand planes in the air multiplied by, let's say one hundred and seventy five."

"Seems fair."

"What's that?" Santa then starts doing some of the math in his head.

"Here," you say, pulling out your phone from your pocket. "Let's just use a calculator."

"Ho, ho, ho," Santa chuckles. "I forget that people always have these things on them now."

You pass your phone over and he hesitantly accepts it from you. "So, I just use it like any other calculator?"

"Yeah, just tap the buttons on the screen."

He's clearly nervous about using this technology. "Okay," he says and starts pressing the screen with his gloved fingers. Nothing happens.

"You probably need to take your gloves off. Unless there is some type of conductive rubber or foam in the fingertips of your gloves, the touchscreen won't work."

"Oh," Santa shakes his head. "I don't take my gloves off until my work is done."

"Really? Why's that?"

"I use my hands a lot at work, be it reigning in my magical reindeer or hauling my very substantial sack of presents. The gloves that I require for this need to be form fitting and yet sturdy. Believe it or not, but it takes me several minutes to take them off."

"I believe it," you say, figuring that the old man must also have at least a minor case of arthritis that would slow him down. "I must ask, then, what are those made of? They are amazingly soft."

"Baby seal skin."

You are unable to disguise your shock. "Really?"

"Oh yes. There's nothing quite like it. You seem surprised?"

"Well, yes."

Santa shakes his head and chuckles again. "Ho, ho, ho. I live in the arctic. Utilizing animal hides is an integral part of life there."

"It's just that the baby seal hunt is such a controversial thing down here."

"Well, I won't judge how the billions of you southerners flagrantly waste so much of your bountiful resources, and you won't judge how the few of us kill a handful animals but use every part of their being in a respectful manner, okay?"

Santa actually seemed a little ticked off there. And, if you're not mistaken, he sure appeared to be judging you, contrary to what he said. But you have no intention of starting an argument with Santa Claus, of all people. You wouldn't want to find your name on the naughty list. "I'm sorry, Santa. I didn't mean to be disrespectful."

"Don't apologize. You're just asking a question." He then looks at the phone in his hand. "So, what should I do with this then?"

"Here," you take it back from him, "it's probably easier if I just do it."

"Good plan."

You then look back to Santa. "What was I calculating again?"

"I forgot."

"Something about air travel."

"Oh, yes. I wanted to estimate the number of passengers in the air at any given time and see how this compares to the general U.S. population."

You snap your fingers in acknowledgement. "That was it. So, what should I type in?"

"Well, five thousand planes multiplied by, what did we figure it was? One hundred and seventy-five people per plane?"

An interesting choice of words, you think. *We* figured. It was all you. But you'll let Santa revel in the joint credit for that one. "Yeah." You type this in. "So, twenty-six thousand two hundred and fifty."

Santa puts the last of the oatmeal-raisin cookie into his mouth. "That's not much compared to three hundred million," he says with slightly garbled consonants.

"Agreed." You then look to the phone in your hand and perform a quick, supplemental calculation. "That's about point zero-zero-nine percent of the American population at any given time."

"Can't see how that seems unreasonable. And, I must say, you sure seem proficient at calculating percentages."

"I guess I'd have to thank my sixth grade teacher."

"Mr. Sturlubok?" Santa asks.

"Wow, you really do know everything."

"If I remember correctly, he was always on my naughty list.

Received a lump of coal every year of his childhood."

"Every single year?"

"I only decide on the consequence, I don't decide on the behavior."

Although you're not at all surprised to learn this—Mr. Sturlubok's irritable nature surely began long before he was an adult—you also figure that Santa's refusal to ever grant the child even a single present in his lifetime might have had something to do with his testy mood. However, you are not about to tell Santa Claus how he should do his job. You then try to recall just why you started estimating the proportion of American citizens in flight at any given time in relation to the total population of the country. "Why were we talking about this, again?"

Santa cocks his head, finishes chewing the last morsels of the oatmeal-raisin cookie, swallows, and then shrugs his shoulders. "You know, I can't remember."

"No harm, either way. It was an interesting conversation."

"Indeed." Santa runs his tongue over his teeth and looks towards the empty bowl of Ann's famous holiday punch. "Actually, could I bother you for something to drink? Those cookies were delicious, but they sure make an old man thirsty."

"Of course." For a moment you feel like a terrible host, neglecting the rather obvious duty of offering your guest a beverage. But then you realize that Santa Claus was never really invited, and is technically trespassing on your property. Of course, you're not bothered by this, but you feel that this fact negates any potential guilt for not getting him a drink earlier. "I'm guessing you'd like a glass of milk?"

"Ho, ho, ho," Santa chuckles, forcing you to look back up the stairs in case any of the doors might open. "That is always a favorite of mine."

You walk over to the fridge, but right as you grip the smooth stainless steel handle (which you notice is covered in an assortment of fingerprints and smears; you really wish Ann would have cleaned this up before going to bed), you turn back to Santa Claus and say, "Actually, I have another idea."

"Oh, what's that?"

"How about instead of milk, I get you a tall glass of Cranberry 7-Up, on the rocks? It's limited edition."

"That's a wonderful idea!" Santa enthuses, "I love both 7-Up and cranberries."

"Maybe it's just me," you say while dropping a couple cubes of ice into a glass, "but I think the two really complement each other." You retrieve a can from the fridge, crack open the tab, and gently pour its sparkling contents against the side of the glass. Leaving only a quarter-inch of room at the top (figuring that Santa is the type of person who wants more than just a few sips of soda), you carefully hand over the glass to Jolly Saint Nick, who grips it with his (baby seal skin) gloves.

He carefully brings the glass to his lips, takes a slurping sip, pauses, smiles, and then exhales a panting sigh of pleasure. "Oh, that is tasty."

There's just no point in resisting any longer. "I'm going to have to join you," you say before getting another glass, a pair of ice cubes, and a second can of Cranberry 7-Up. In less time than it takes a kid to tear apart the wrapping on a Christmas present, you have your own fizzing glass and tap it against Santa's. "Cheers."

"Cheers."

After a few (devilishly refreshing) sips from your drink, you put down your beverage and say, "So, I'm not sure if you can tell me, but I've just got to ask something."

"What's that?"

"How do you do it? How do you manage to visit all the homes in the world, all with such a short time frame? I mean, regardless of all the logistics of getting in and out of so many chimneys—"

Santa interrupts, "—I don't actually use chimneys, you should know."

"Really?"

"No, of course not. It made sense back in Victorian times, but not now. You guys don't even have a chimney. Your fireplace burns natural gas."

"Then how did you get in here?"

"Your patio door."

"Huh."

"Is that really any more surprising than the idea of me going through a chimney?"

"Not really."

"But, anyhow, I apologize for interrupting. You were saying?"

"Oh, yes. I was saying, regardless of all the logistics of getting into people's homes and dropping off the presents, how do you travel from location to location so quickly and yet not break the sound barrier? I figure you'd have to be going *at least* five to ten-times the speed of sound, and yet I've never heard a single sonic boom in all the many nights before Christmas."

"Ho, ho, ho! Imagine all the ruckus that would cause? Every child in the world would be awoken in the middle of the night."

You think of telling Santa that your children are going to be awoken in the middle of the night should he continue to laugh with such volume. It's easy for Santa to be so jolly—he doesn't have to deal with the consequences of two cranky, sleep-deprived children for an entire day. "So, how do you do it then?"

Santa grins. "You want me to tell you?"

"Yes, please. I just can't get my head around how it's possible."

"It's really quite simple, actually."

"Well?"

Santa leans close and after a dramatic pause, he whispers:

"Magic."

That seems like a bit of a cop-out. But you're not about to relay this thought to Santa Claus (again: naughty list), so you nod and say, "Ahhh. I see. When you put it like that, it really is simple."

"So," Santa chugs back the rest of his Cranberry 7-Up, raising the bottom of the glass high enough so that the ice cubes clatter against his lips. You've barely made a dent in your drink. That man likes his soda, you think. You then wonder if he should be tested for type II diabetes. However, if he can use the catch-all solution of *magic* to take care of all the details regarding delivering presents to billions of children in a single night, then surely he can also use this same magic to control his blood-sugar levels. "As much as I'd like to spend my entire night here chatting with you, I do have a job to do."

"Oh, yeah. I guess you're on shift right now."

"Indeed," Santa then pulls up a great burlap sack that had been resting on the floor. "I have some presents I need to put under that beautiful Christmas tree of yours." He heaves the bag over one shoulder and walks through the living room, leaving watery prints along your oak hardwood floors. Although you can't be surprised that he doesn't take off his boots (considering he won't even take off his gloves), you really wish he might have wiped them off at the patio mat. He groans while putting down the bag and loosens a string around the opening. "The first one here is for little Liam," he says while retrieving a present wrapped in a glossy, baby-blue wrapping paper, topped with a perfect white bow. He passes it over to you, "What do you think this might be?"

As you grab the box to give it a shake, you are surprised to notice that the bow is just a sticker. Perhaps naively, you assumed that Santa would be above such things. You shake the package and something rolls against the sides of the box. Another jiggle and you feel confident. "It's a toy truck, isn't it?"

"Ho, ho, ho!" Santa laughs, "You've had some practice at this, haven't you?"

You hand the gift back and Santa lays it down on the ground. He then returns to his bag and withdraws a similarly-sized box (although a little more square at one end), this decorated in a sparkling pink wrapping paper "This must be for Emma?" You ask, and Santa nods. Shaking this box doesn't seem to do anything, but then you feel a gentle thud. Applying a little more force, you can tell that one side is heavier. "Hmm, this is a little more tricky."

"What's your guess?"

"It's not a phone, is it? Emma keeps pestering us for one, but I really want to hold off on her having a phone for at least another year or two. Although, I will admit it would give Ann and I a little more peace of mind for when she's not at home. I could activate the 'find-my-phone' feature and see where she is at any given time."

"No, it's not a phone."

"Good," you say with relief, but also a slight tinge of disappointment. Now that you think about it, Santa bringing Emma a phone would really save you hundreds of dollars. And there would be nothing stopping you from holding onto the present for a year or two. "So, what is it?"

"It's a doll!" Santa says with a beaming grin.

"Oh," you force out a smile. Santa Claus is really all in with the gender stereotypes, it appears. Honestly, you can't think of the last time that you saw Emma play with such a toy. "That's so nice."

"She's going to love it, isn't she?"

"Oh, yes."

He places Emma's present beneath the tree and returns to his bag. "Now, I don't usually do this for grown-ups," he says while rummaging through the unseen packages, "but I have one for you, as well." He pulls out another gift, smaller than the others, and holds it out for you to take.

"This is for me?"

"Yes, yes, yes."

The present has almost no weight. When you shake it, it seems to be empty. Is Santa's gift some sort of metaphor? Is he saying that your life is already so full and exciting that you don't need anything else? If this is the case, you'd rather he just tell you as much, not package an empty box under the guise of a Christmas present.

He asks, "Any idea what it is?"

"It seems empty."

"Ho, ho, ho! It's not empty."

Good. But whatever it is, it will be impossible to figure out just by rattling the package. "I have no idea." You then turn to place the present beneath the tree with the others.

"Oh," Santa says, "you don't need to do that. You can open it now."

"I can?"

"It is Christmas morning, is it not?"

Considering that both of his gifts for your children were somewhat underwhelming, you have to feign an excited smile. "Really?"

"Yes, yes, yes. Go ahead. See what's inside."

"Well, if you say so." You start by peeling off the white bow and look for somewhere to put it.

Santa reaches out, "I'll take that. I try to reuse them as much as possible."

While you can't fault the man for being frugal, you wonder if he realizes that you can now buy great bags of these things for just a few bucks at any dollar store? Chances are, Santa doesn't appreciate how the manufacturing power of China has made items like this so much more affordable. "Here you go," you pass Santa the bow and look for a seam in the glossy paper to pull apart. The wrapping job is amazing. Every line is ruler straight. Every fold is crisp, perfect 90-degree angles. The paper is taut. The corners are sharp. It almost seems to be a shame to wreck this (especially since you're not convinced that Santa really got you an exceptional present). You tug at one edge and pull apart a strip of tape. Taking care to unfold—not tear—you open one side of the decorative paper and expose a plain white box with a square lid. It has no markings of any type. You look back up to Santa Claus, as if to seek permission to go further.

"Go ahead, then." Santa says. "Take a look at what's inside."

Lifting the top reveals a single garment. It is a pair of children's underwear, white fabric with an assortment of colorful dinosaur silhouettes. You hold it up, force a toothy smile and say the only thing you can think of. "Thanks."

"Well? What do you think they are?"

"Underwear for Liam?"

"Yes," Santa says, expecting you to add more.

You aren't sure what else there is to say. "I think we actually have the exact same pair. But thank you, anyhow. One can never have enough children's clothes, right?"

"Ho, ho, ho!" Santa shakes his head and pats his belly. "Don't you see?"

Looking at the tiny garment again, you aren't sure what is so special about this. "No. We have this already." You then have a crazy thought. A wonderful thought. A thought so seemingly preposterous that you are nervous about admitting it to Santa Claus.

"Well?" Santa prods.

"Are you saying that Liam is toilet trained?"

"Exactly," Santa winks. "Starting today, you'll be needing those a lot more."

"So, just to be clear, are these magic undies that Liam will need to wear in order to avoid being incontinent?"

"No," Santa pats you on the shoulder. "They are just a symbol. I didn't realize that Liam already has that pair. I just figured he might like those because of the dinosaurs on them. Boys love dinosaurs."

"I don't know what to say, Santa." You shake your head in disbelief.

"I believe the words you're looking for are: *Merry Christmas!*" Santa bellows before breaking into his signature, booming laugh.

You hate to do this, especially after being given such a perfect Christmas gift, but you really don't want to wake up the kids right now. "Actually, Santa. I'm really sorry, but I think you might wake up Liam and Emma if you keep laughing so loud. It's just, once they are up, they don't go back down, and then everyone has to be up, and then everyone is tired, and then everyone ends up in a bad mood, and all around it leads to a really, really long day."

Santa stares at you with a coy expression.

"What?" you say.

"You do realize that this is all a dream, right?"

"Oh." Of course. There is no way that *Wonderful Christmastime* would play three times in a single evening on the same satellite radio station. Suddenly, this gift in your hands feels like a trick. "Yeah."

Santa then says, "Or is it?"

"What?"

Santa laughs.

You really wish Santa Claus would be a little more direct. "Are you now saying that this is *not* a dream?"

"I already told you that this is a dream."

"Oh. So, I guess that Liam isn't really toilet trained, is he?"

Santa winks at you.

You ask, "What does that mean?"

"It means whatever you want it to mean."

"What?"

Santa winks again.

"I'm really confused."

"And I really need to get going. There are a lot of boys and girls

129

out there that still need their presents.”

“Can you just tell me, straight up, if Liam is toilet trained or not?”

“You’ll have to just wake up in the morning and find out.”

“You said, ‘Wake up.’ So, you’re implying that this is just a dream?”

With one hand on your shoulder, Santa guides you back towards the sofa. “You’ve had a long day. You should get some more rest.”

“So, I’m awake right now?”

Again, Santa winks. To be honest, you find it almost infuriating. But you don’t resist as he directs you back down. He says, “You’ve had a lot to drink tonight. Ann’s famous holiday punch is great, but they go down too easy.”

“Ain’t that the truth,” you say, your eyelids now heavy.

“Merry Christmas,” Santa says as he walks away.

“Merry Christmas,” you say with heavy lips, listening to Santa’s plodding steps, the opening and closing of the patio door, and then his lumbering gait along the wooden deck. You still have that pair of Liam’s underwear in your hands, but instead of letting it go, you roll over and keep it snug by your chest. As you easily drift back off into sleep (although unsure if you are already asleep and this is just part of an imaginary slumber), you can’t help but think, even if all of this isn’t real—even if you wake up in a few hours and Liam demands a diaper change like every other morning—then it will still be a fine day, because it will be *Christmas Day*. Because there will be cinnamon buns for breakfast. Because you’ll eat chocolate before ten in the morning. Because you’ll get to enjoy a can of limited edition Cranberry 7-Up any time you wish (and in the afternoon it *will* be spiked with vodka). Because Ann can surely be cajoled into making another batch of oatmeal-raisin cookies. Because if you need to drive somewhere, the roads will be free from traffic. And because, more than anything else, it will be a day to spend time with your family. Or did you think that already? Although you can't be sure, you feel quite certain that it must have been one of the first things that came to your mind.

The End

■ ■ ■

IF YOU ENJOYED THIS BOOK (WOULDN'T THAT BE IRONIC?) PLEASE REVIEW IT AT AMAZON.COM. IT HELPS.

ABOUT THE AUTHOR

Rudolf Kerkhoven lives a very boring life with his wife and two children in the Vancouver area of British Columbia. He has a membership to Costco. And he has a soft spot for *Wonderful Christmastime.*

www.RudolfKerkhoven.com

@BownessBooks